LAURA SPIVAK

When Evelyn Daydreams

Bear Pond
PRESS

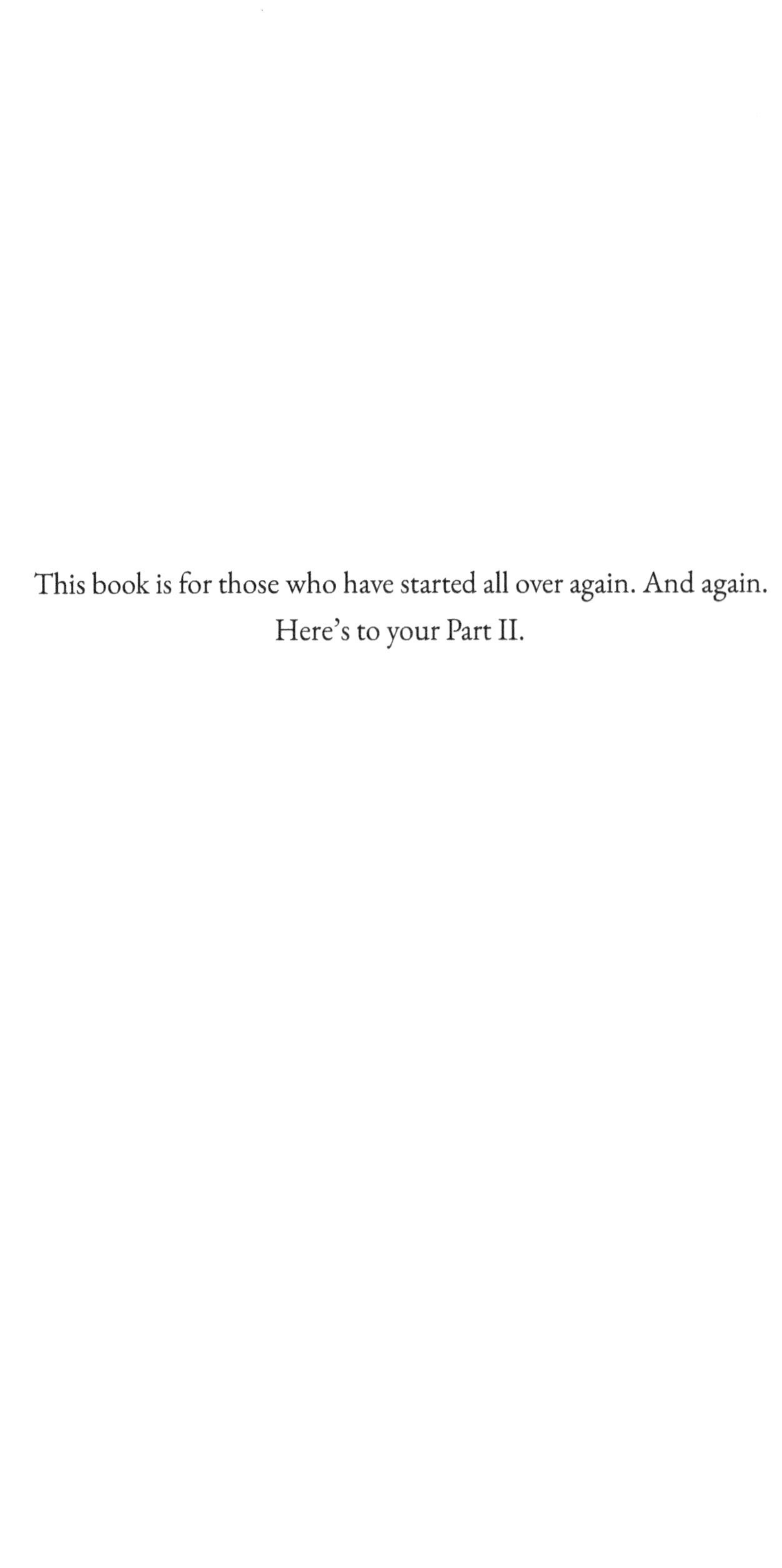

This book is for those who have started all over again. And again. Here's to your Part II.

Chapter 1
2006

Alone on a bench in Washington Square Park, Will Jenkins stared at the weathered piece of paper in his hand. It had been folded and unfolded so many times it was starting to fall apart, but he still carried it everywhere. He'd memorized every stroke of her pen, every word, every tear-stained blot. They were all pieces of her. He took a deep breath as he reread the words he knew by heart. The words she'd written to him so long ago as she'd prepared to die and leave him behind.

Will,

Writing this letter is one of the hardest things I have ever had to do. I have so little time to say so much. No letter could ever contain the feelings I have for you, but with every second ticking closer to my death, I'll try.

You came into my life at a time when my idea of happiness was warped and contrived. I'd forced myself to be happy in situations that weren't meant for me. Knowing you has helped me learn I was accepting less than I was worth. I'll never be able to adequately thank you for showing me what it is to be truly loved.

Our time together will never have been long enough, but somehow, it's as if I've been with you forever. You know me better than I know myself.

I used to think of my other timeline as an escape, but once I met you, I didn't want to escape anymore. You are my peace.

When I'm gone, I want you to take our love and spread it. With someone new. Spread it all over the city and the world, as far as you can. Make people happy. Make their lives better. That's all we ever wanted when we met protesting for a war to end, wasn't it? For peoples' lives to be better?

You made my life better, Will. I will never forget that or any of the beautiful moments we shared. Wherever I am, whenever I am, I will always be grateful for the way you showed me how to soften myself and open my heart to the idea of love as it really is. Not a day will go by when I won't think of you on the other side.

I'll visit you at our park, my love.
Your Dream Girl,
Evelyn

As he folded the letter and put it back into his pocket, Will sighed deeply and looked up at the fiery leaves in the trees. This time of year reminded him of Evelyn. They'd started dating in the fall. He imagined her sitting on this very bench next to him, laughing with him as they cracked jokes and basked in each other's company. He'd come to this place often since she passed away, trying to relive even a fraction of what they'd had, but it just wasn't the same without her. Nothing was.

It had been three years since Evelyn had died in his arms. She was gone, and he was stuck while the rest of the world moved on. It didn't help that in the time since Evelyn had passed, Will's mother had also been taken from him by a sudden and nasty bout of bronchitis-turned-pneumonia. His mother was all Will had left after Evelyn, and the consecutive losses had sent him reeling.

He had never been able to talk to anyone honestly about Evelyn's death because there was no good way to tell people your girlfriend died when she lost the ability to time travel in her sleep and she'd gone to permanently live in an alternate timeline eighty-four years in the past. But that's what had happened. And he'd been in a constant state of disarray ever since, trying to come to terms with the unbelievable things he'd experienced.

He reached into his coat and pulled out an airplane bottle of rum. He contemplated pouring it into his coffee, but he had to be at work in twenty minutes. He sighed deeply and put the bottle back into his pocket. He read Evelyn's letter again instead.

Chapter 2

1922

Evelyn stood in the same spot, in the same park, at the same time as Will, eighty-four years before him. She swore she could sometimes feel him there when she visited. It had been their place. A tinge of guilt washed over her for what seemed like the millionth time, and she chided herself for still thinking about Will when she was officially engaged to Thomas here in 1922. As much as she'd tried to put it aside, it had been harder to move on from 2003 than she'd ever imagined.

Thomas had been an amazing support for her as she grieved the loss of an entire life when she stopped traveling to her other timeline in her sleep, but he could never understand how hard it had been for her to lose Will. The love she shared with Thomas in this life was a fulfilling, reliable, wholesome love that bolstered her when she was weak and made the happy times even more joyous. It was what she needed here.

What she'd had with Will in 2003 was natural, effortless, and warm. He had understood her so completely in a way she'd never experienced with another person. Being with him had made her strong. It was as if nothing could break her as long as they were together. She'd once told him he was the love of both her lives, and though she would never admit it out loud in this timeline, he still was.

Evelyn raised her brow at a particularly tame squirrel that had appeared in front of her and was staring her in the eye. "I know, I know. I need to get going." The creature scampered away when she got up.

Thomas was due to come over to her apartment after work. She'd spent the day house hunting alone. He had planned to join her, but he'd stopped by and informed her last night that he wouldn't be able to come. Opening a new psychotherapy practice was taking up all Thomas's time lately, and Evelyn found herself doing everything else alone while he worked.

Thomas was starting his venture alongside Karl, a German psychiatrist who had recently moved to the United States, to expand his horizons in the rapidly emerging field of psychology. The two had been immersed in the business for weeks, and while Evelyn was immeasurably proud of her fiancé for being a frontrunner in his profession, she was craving more time with him. A lump formed in her throat as she quietly admitted to herself that, more than anything, her heart was aching for companionship.

In the last year or so, her core group of girlfriends had stopped spending as much time together. It wasn't by choice. Lily had moved to Queens with her new husband, George, after a whirlwind romance. He was an entrepreneur who was opening a delicatessen there, so it wasn't often that Lily made it back to Manhattan for a brunch with the group. Emily had started secretarial school and was working at the makeup counter in the Lord and Taylor flagship store to pay for her schooling, which left little time in her schedule for socializing. Evelyn still saw Ada sometimes, but it just hadn't been the same since their heyday. Between losing time with her friends and now Thomas, Evelyn was spending so much time by herself it was starting to gnaw at her.

She was increasingly regretting her decision to quit her job as a legal secretary in order to prepare for the wedding and settle into a new home. Aside from the fact that very little wedding planning had taken place because Thomas was consumed with his work, Evelyn missed getting up every day and going to the office to do something that mattered beyond her own life. There had been moments lately when resentment overwhelmed her, and she lashed out at Thomas for ever suggesting she take time off work. The truth was she was bristling with anger at herself for agreeing to it in the first place.

Work, her relationship, and money were certainly stressors and worthy of her attention, but Evelyn was harboring something that trumped them all, and she hadn't told a soul what it was. It occupied her thoughts day and night, and she was aching to unburden herself of the information. More than that, she had to find out what revelations it may bring.

As she walked home, she kept her eyes peeled for the person she'd been keeping from Thomas—and everyone else—for months. Evelyn had spotted a man who looked *exactly* like Will. She'd made direct eye contact with him several times, but he showed no signs of recognizing her. A few times she'd wondered if she was imagining it and if maybe she needed to ask Thomas to help find her a psychotherapist of her own. Instead she'd kept Will's doppelgänger a closely guarded secret, only recording in a private journal every time and place she'd seen the man who looked every bit like her greatest love. She didn't know if the records would ever be helpful or not, but she'd relied on writing things down her entire life and figured the logs might come in handy when she eventually got up the courage to ask her friend Doctor Holstead to help her identify the man who had been haunting her.

Evelyn didn't have to wait long to see Doctor Holstead. Thomas had invited him to join them for dinner. It wasn't uncommon. Holstead was a dear friend, and he had been instrumental in helping them both navigate the loss of Evelyn's dream life three years ago. He and his caregiver, Mrs. Brooks, were always welcome guests in Evelyn's home and were like family by now. Recently, Evelyn had become a little uneasy around them because she knew they would inevitably ask about the wedding and whether they'd gotten any closer to finding a new home, and she didn't want to explain that both topics had been the source of some rather heated fights in her relationship of late. She talked around their questions over dinner, changing the subject when she could. Grateful when the main course ended, she gathered the empty plates and took them into the kitchen. She was exhausted from a day of walking around the city and keeping secrets. Thankful for a moment to herself, she leaned over the counter, closed her eyes, and took a deep breath.

"My dear, are you quite all right?"

Evelyn jumped at the unexpected question from Doctor Holstead.

"I'm sorry. I didn't mean to startle you."

"No, I'm fine," Evelyn assured him, her hand on her chest as she steadied her breathing. "I'm actually glad to have a moment to chat with you alone."

"Oh?" He raised his eyebrows, intrigued.

Evelyn glanced through the kitchen door, making sure Thomas and Mrs. Brooks were suitably distracted with their own conversation before she spoke.

"I have something to tell you, and it might sound strange," she began, "but you're the only person I can talk to about it. The only one who might be able to help."

Concerned, Holstead placed his hand on her forehead. "You're not sick, are you?"

"No, nothing like that." Evelyn shook her head. "It's to do with my dreams."

He lowered his arm, his eyes wide. "They're not back, are they?"

Sudden sadness made Evelyn's stomach tighten. She wished that were the case.

"No." She gazed at the floor. Evelyn hadn't had a dream since she'd lost her 2003 timeline. Her nights were spent in darkness. No time travel. No regular dreams—not that she'd ever had a regular dream. Just eerie nothingness. But that wasn't what she needed to talk to Holstead about. She looked him in the eye and uttered her secret aloud for the very first time. "There's a man. I don't know who he is, but I've been spotting him all over the city for months." She paused when Holstead's expression changed. She quickly clarified. "He looks *just* like Will, my boyfriend from 2003."

Holstead was silent, clearly unsure of what she was asking of him.

"I need to find out who that man is," Evelyn explained as she picked up a dish towel and wrung it in her hands. "I can't help feeling like I need to talk to him. I have to know his name. It's eating me alive."

"My dear, I know you loved that boy, but you must know it's not possible for this to be him." Holstead's tone hinted to Evelyn that he thought she might be seeing things.

"I know." She stared down at the rag in her hands. "I don't know what I'm expecting. I just can't let go of the idea that I'm meant to meet the man who looks like Will. To talk to him."

"I suppose telling Thomas about this lookalike would be a bit of a thorn in your relationship, so I can see why you wouldn't want to tell him," Holstead acknowledged. "But why are you telling *me*? How can I help?"

"I was wondering if you could look through your research and find out if this happened to any of the other dreamers. Seeing lookalikes from their other lives after they'd stopped traveling between timelines?

Something's telling me there's more to the dreams. That they're not really over yet."

"I can't recall any of our subjects having that after-effect, but I'll see what I can find."

She put the dish towel on the counter and hugged him. "Thank you." Letting him go, she picked up a large plate of confections she'd put together earlier for dessert. Facing him again, she smiled. "Shall we?"

Chapter 3

2006

Will stared through his office window at the flags of the world flying outside the United Nations building. His mind wandered to the day in 2003 when he and Evelyn had led an anti-war protest together among those flagpoles. The way the evening sun had glinted off her blonde hair as she handed out pamphlets to passersby. The determination in her stride as she'd worked to make a real difference in the world.   He was snapped out of his thoughts by his boss, Jamie, who tapped on the doorframe with his wedding band as he entered to deliver some paperwork to Will's desk. Will attempted to appear busy, but it was clear he had not been actively working. It wasn't the first time this week or even today he'd been caught off-task, and Will wondered how much more patience his boss had left for his dwindling performance of late.

Jamie placed the papers on Will's desk, disappointment and frustration written on his face. "If you don't mind getting these back to me as soon as you can," he said, turning to leave. "Thanks."

Will sighed, angry for once again allowing himself to be caught focusing on his past instead of working hard to secure his present and future. He'd landed his dream job at the UN after graduation, and though it should have been one of the proudest accomplishments of his life, it was overshadowed by the one-two punch of his unbearable losses.

In the days after Evelyn died, Will had been numb. He found it hard to cry or show any hint of the intense emotions that were billowing beneath the shock of her death. It had all been such a whirlwind. The funeral, the visitors, the endless condolences and pitiful looks. His mother had come from Ohio to stay with him for a few weeks after Evelyn passed. It had been strange for Will to let his mom take care of him after so many years of him making sure she was okay, but her presence had been the one thing that kept him afloat after he lost Evelyn, and he would be forever grateful for those few weeks. After his mother had left and everything calmed down, Will had more time to sit with himself and begin to process his emotions. Evelyn hadn't just been a girlfriend. She was the love of his life and his soulmate. He knew with everything in him he would never find another love that could rival what they'd shared. He found himself at the beginning of a downward spiral.

He'd managed to keep his studies on track somehow and graduated college with honors. He had majored in political science and minored in psychology. But in the background of that success, he had been treading water emotionally and mentally. He couldn't get Evelyn out of his head, and thoughts of how he might have done things differently to save her consumed his every waking moment.

"Stop daydreaming and do your work," Will whispered to himself, rubbing his hands over his face to center his thoughts and switch gears. He picked up the paperwork Jamie had dropped off and busied himself with it, anxiously checking the time every few minutes until he could finally leave the office. He pushed in his chair and crept out of the office and into the elevator before his boss could give him anything more to do. Guilt always ate at him when he rushed out of work without saying anything to his boss, but there was only one thing that helped him numb all the pain he was drowning in on days like this, when the memories were like an endless, heartbreaking hamster wheel inside his brain.

After a short, brisk walk down the block, Will descended a flight of concrete steps that led to the entrance of a basement bar called Chasers. He had first come to the bar one day after work, when the "what ifs" that haunted him every day had been particularly relentless. What if he had done more research into Evelyn's dreams and had been able to find the cure that could have kept her here? What if he'd never transferred to school in New York and he'd been home to take care of his mother? He couldn't help but blame himself for losing the two most important people in his life, and a quick shot or two seemed to help suppress the whirlwind of self-deprecation that took over his mind every night when the lights went out.

The truth was Will's depression was making it increasingly difficult to get out of bed and get to work on time, find the motivation to tidy up his living space, or cook healthy meals for himself. He knew if he didn't stop getting to work late and underperforming, his job might be the next thing he lost. He wanted so badly to stop stuffing his feelings down but knew, if he allowed the grief to fully consume him, it would be the worst pain of his life. Stuck in emotional limbo, Will found himself powerless to let go and fully accept the pain of Evelyn's nonexistence and the fact that he was now an orphan. He wasn't sure he could survive it.

When he did drink, he did it alone. He had never run into anyone he knew at Chasers, which suited him just fine. The only familiar faces were the ones who worked there, and Will had been a frequent-enough customer lately that they were all on a first-name basis with him. He was too depressed to be embarrassed about it, but Max, who was the usual bartender when Will was there, had recently given him the name and phone number of his sister's therapy practice and suggested Will call and make an appointment.

"It's not that I think you're drinking too much; you only have a couple when you come in," Max had said. "It's just . . . look, I know it's not my business, but I can see how tough all this has been on you. Losing your girlfriend and then your mom would be a lot for anyone. I'm just trying to help."

Max's heart was in the right place, but Will simply didn't have the motivation to follow his advice.

As he plopped down into his regular seat at the bar, Will ordered a Coors Light from Max, who, without a word, quickly returned with the frosty bottle along with a small glass of champagne. Will took the champagne and stared at the bubbles floating from the bottom of the glass in orderly lines before he tipped his glass to the bartender and threw back the entire drink. Champagne had been Evelyn's favorite.

"Thanks," Will said, handing the empty glass back to Max.

"To Evelyn, right?" Max wiped a few drops of champagne off the bartop.

"To Evelyn."

Chapter 4

2006

Will emerged from the stairwell of Chasers, gripping the rusty handrail as he went. The bright lights of the city street were a lot to handle after the comforting dimness of the bar, and he squinted as he made his way to the curb. As he raised his arm to hail a cab, he caught sight of a dark-haired woman in pale green scrubs coming toward him on the sidewalk. Their eyes met, and she instantly perked up when she recognized him.

"Will! Hey!" Cammie greeted him with a warm hug. Evelyn's best friend had become one of the only people Will talked to outside of work these days. She checked in on him often, which he appreciated more than she probably knew. No one else really asked him how he was doing anymore, as if there was some deadline on grieving that had already passed. But Cammie never acted like his losses hadn't happened. She called or sent him a text message every week or two, and sometimes they met up for coffee or lunch. They didn't always talk about Evelyn, but if he was having an unusually tough day or he needed to vent, Cammie was a reliable sounding board.

She glanced at the flickering neon sign above the stairs, and Will instantly blushed.

"You coming from work?" He started walking away from Chasers, and she followed.

"Yeah," Cammie said, tucking her hair behind her ear. "I just worked a double shift. I was hoping to run into a handsome, single diplomat on my way home, but I guess you'll do." She winked at him and smiled.

She lived only a few blocks from the UN Building, and they had a running joke that Will would someday use his professional connections to introduce her to an eligible foreign bachelor making a political visit to the US, but the truth was, Will hadn't worked hard enough at his job recently to advance to the point where he was face-to-face with the diplomats. "I was just about to head home, but I haven't seen a cab." He turned back toward the street to look again for a taxi and lost his footing, stumbling off the curb. Cammie reached out and grabbed his elbow to help steady him.

"Do you wanna share a cab?" She let go of him when he stepped back up onto the sidewalk.

Will's defenses immediately spiked at the suggestion that he was too inebriated to go home alone. "I'm not that drunk. I just fell."

"I know! I wasn't saying you're wasted or anything. I just figured we could catch up while we rode together."

Will gazed past her at the flashing bar sign. "Actually, I could use some company. Wanna stop by my place and hang out for a bit?"

Fifteen minutes later, the two entered Will's apartment. He made his way into the kitchen and pulled a can of beer from the almost-empty fridge. Cammie swooped in and took it from him, switching it for a bottle of water from her work bag. "I think this is what you really need," she said, opening it and handing it back.

She was right. He had work in the morning. Will muttered his thanks to her and chugged almost the whole bottle in one go.

When he finished it, he put the bottle in the recycling bin and noticed the overflowing garbage receptacle beside it. Looking around his living room, he was embarrassed at how he'd been living. Clothes strewn all over the furniture and floor, takeout containers sitting on the living room table, and a few empty beer bottles scattered throughout the space. Moving boxes he'd never unpacked littered every corner. They'd become extra surfaces on which he'd piled unopened mail and other clutter. Cammie's eyes widened as she took in her surroundings, and Will wished he'd had the motivation to clean up in the last few weeks. He just hadn't. "Sorry about the mess," he said, scratching the back of his head. "I guess I've been a little down lately."

"That's okay," Cammie said, shifting a sweatshirt out of the way to make space for herself on the couch. "I can help clean up a little if you want?"

"No, that's okay. I mean, I should clean up my own mess. You relax. I'm gonna go change out of my work clothes. I'll be right back."

He closed his bedroom door behind him and began rifling through his dresser drawers. He scolded himself when he saw he was running dangerously low on clean laundry and vowed to get himself together in the next few days and clean up his apartment.

Once he'd pulled on a pair of jeans and a T-shirt, he returned to the living room where Cammie was wiping her eyes as she held a photograph in her hands.

"I miss her, too," he said quietly.

Cammie eased down onto the couch, her eyes glued to the photo.

"I still can't look at pictures of her without getting sad." She ran her fingers over her best friend's haunting image.

"Yeah." He didn't need to say anything else. He was buzzed, but he knew she understood.

A single tear escaped her eye and made its way down her cheek. "Evelyn was such a good person." Cammie smiled softly through her heartache. "She didn't deserve to die so young."

"I should have saved her."

Cammie's head snapped toward him. "Will, there was nothing you could have done. You know that, right?"

He stared at the photo as he sat down next to her, silent.

"You couldn't have saved her. You have to stop blaming yourself," Cammie reiterated as if reading his thoughts.

"That's what everyone says." He scoffed. "I was the *only* one who could have saved her."

"How do you think I feel? I was studying to be a nurse, and I didn't even know anything was wrong with my best friend!"

They sat in silence for a few strained moments, unsure of what to do or say next.

"Okay, that's enough," Cammie said suddenly, grabbing his arm. "Evelyn wouldn't have wanted us to be this sad for so long. Let's cheer up, okay?"

He stared into Cammie's eyes, and for the first time he felt someone else realized the absolute depths of his sorrow. He was broken, and she recognized in him her own deep pain over losing Evelyn. Something about the mutual understanding they shared in that moment drew them to each other like magnets, and before Will knew what he was doing, his lips were on hers. It happened so fast he didn't have time to process whether it was a good or bad idea, and once he'd started kissing her, something in him couldn't stop. He allowed himself to give in, free of overthinking everything for a few blissful moments, before he finally pulled himself away. They locked eyes as they each caught their breath, stunned silent over what they'd just done.

"I shouldn't have done that. I'm sorry," she eventually blurted out as she stood and ran to retrieve her bag from the kitchen counter. "I have to go."

Cammie didn't give him a chance to respond. She closed the door behind her.

Chapter 5

1922

Evelyn had left home early to go to another apartment showing. The place, like all the others she'd looked at for Thomas and herself, was too expensive for them with his practice not open yet, and she was growing weary of touring the endless string of homes that were out of their reach. They could move into Thomas's family home, but he didn't want to live with his mother as a married man, and Evelyn had to admit she would rather be alone with her new husband as well. She wished Thomas would agree to just move into her apartment after the wedding. It had previously belonged to her great aunt, who had left it to Evelyn's parents in her will. It wasn't very big, but the two of them could comfortably live there until they had their feet under them financially. Instead, Thomas's idea was to rent it out and use the money to help fund a larger place for them to live in. Evelyn hated the idea of giving up her apartment. Women in New York in 1922 did not commonly have their own places, and she'd enjoyed the sense of independence and power it had afforded her. If only she could get Thomas to see reason. He was insistent that they should find a place closer to his new office, and one big enough to be home to a future child, which they agreed they wanted someday. At present, Evelyn felt like they were so far away from having a family it was laughable, but the way Thomas lit up when he talked about children was worth the aggravation of at least trying to find a new place to live, so she'd agreed to diligently search for one.

After a frustrating morning, Evelyn met with her good friend Ada to break up her day a bit, and she was glad to have someone to talk to. She hadn't opened up much to anyone about the problems she was having in her relationship, and she needed to get some things off her chest. By the time she arrived outside the building where Ada worked as a nanny, Evelyn was bursting to talk everything over. Ada eventually emerged and flashed a wide grin at her friend. They hadn't seen each other in a few weeks.

"What a beautiful day!" Ada exclaimed, taking in the crisp autumn sunshine. "I have an hour before I need to be back. Where to?"

"The park?"

The two started down the street. Evelyn had so much she wanted to say, but she was having a hard time figuring out where to begin, so she stayed mostly silent.

After a few minutes, Ada grabbed Evelyn's arm and stopped her from walking further. "Are you going to tell me what's bothering you, or am I going to have to pull it out of you?"

Evelyn forced a laugh. "How do you know something's bothering me?"

"Oh, come on. I know you better than that!"

Evelyn shrugged. "Fine, I confess. I am having some . . . troubles."

"Is it Thomas?"

"Things are complicated right now."

"Things are always complicated when you're planning a wedding."

"That's just it. We're *not* planning a wedding."

"What do you mean?"

Evelyn sighed. "He works all the time. I know he has to, and I don't fault him for it. It's just that I spend so much time by myself. I'm expected to take care of wedding planning, house hunting, and our social life. I barely see him, and when I do, we're always with other people. It's like he's off in another world, and I'm just struggling to run along after him."

"Have you talked to him about it?"

"I've tried. It always ends in an argument. His work is important. I know that. I just didn't know I'd be sharing my husband with his other love: his job."

"I had no idea. I'm sorry, Ev." Ada started walking again and Evelyn followed, waiting for some words of wisdom for her friend. "I'm sure you'll work it out. Thomas adores you. He'd do anything for you."

"I know he loves me. I just sometimes wonder if that's enough or if he is simply too practical to make sense of my feelings. He's a brilliant psychologist, but the only person he can't seem to read is me."

"What could he do to make it better?"

Evelyn pondered the question. "I have been thinking about going back to work, but I haven't had the heart to tell him."

"Why not? I'm sure he would understand. You loved working!"

"He's so excited about getting married and moving and starting his practice. I worry if I go back to work, he'll think I don't want those same things. And I do want a lot of them. It's just that I also need something for myself. I've never had everything in my life tied to a man before. I think maybe I miss having something just for me."

"You've always had an independent streak, Evelyn. Thomas knew that when he fell in love with you. In fact, I think it's one of the reasons *why* he fell in love with you. You can be honest with him about this without hurting him."

Ada was right. Thomas would probably support her going back to work, but Evelyn knew if she did, it would further delay wedding planning, and she wasn't prepared to put that off more than Thomas already had.

The two caught up more as they strolled through Washington Square Park. Evelyn struggled to keep her mind from wandering to Will, but this place made it difficult. Everything in the park reminded her of him. She pondered whether any of the same benches or paving stones here had survived all the way until 2003, and if they could ever be sitting on the same bench at the same time. Did he still come to the park to remember her, or had he moved on and stopped visiting? And why did both possibilities break her heart?

Evelyn reminded herself to pay attention to her friend. They made a promise to try and get together with the rest of the girls for brunch soon, then Evelyn dropped Ada off at work and headed home. As she continued to quietly contemplate what to do about her problems with Thomas, her thoughts strayed to all the secrets she was keeping from him. She couldn't get Doctor Holstead's words out of her head. He hadn't been wrong when he'd warned her that delving into the mystery of Will's lookalike could be troublesome for her relationship, but Evelyn couldn't marry Thomas, or even love him with her whole heart the way she wanted to, until she found out who the doppelgänger was and whether the saga of her time-traveling dreams was truly over. If it wasn't, the implications would be just as big for Thomas as they were for her.

Evelyn stopped cold when, as if summoned out of her thoughts, the lookalike appeared. She held her breath as the man descended the stairs outside the large bank building across the street from where she stood. Every time she saw him, she thought she might faint. He had Will's eyes, his hair, and his tall, slender build. Even his walk. She could imagine him opening his mouth to speak and Will's voice coming out of it. It was the one sound she'd been longing to hear again during all these years. Holstead had reminded her there was no way it could be Will, and he was right, but something in her took over, and before she could talk herself out of it, Evelyn was speeding across the street to catch up to the man who looked like her long-lost love. She had no idea what she was going to say to him, but she absolutely could not let another opportunity go by without finding out who he was.

He was walking fairly quickly, and his long legs were stiff competition for Evelyn, who was not tall and wearing heeled shoes. She managed to catch up to him about half a block later and breathlessly called out from behind him. "Sir! Excuse me, sir!"

The man stopped and turned around. This was the closest Evelyn had ever been to him, and she almost couldn't speak when she saw his face. It could have been Will himself. She had to stop herself from lunging at him and embracing him in tears.

"Can I help you?"

Evelyn, still panting from running after him, scrambled for something to say. "I am so sorry to approach you in the street like this, but I've seen you around the city a few times recently and I can't help feeling that I know you from somewhere. Have we met?"

The man studied her face, and his forehead wrinkled as he thought about where he may have met Evelyn before.

"I work at the bank," he said, pointing to the large building behind them. "Is your husband a client?"

"No." Evelyn blushed at the idea that she was married, given all the current barriers in her way to arriving at the altar. "I don't think that's it."

"I'm sorry, but I can't quite place it, either. I only moved to the city a few months ago from Ohio, so I don't know very many people here yet. What's your name?"

"Evelyn Moore," she answered, glad the ruse was working so far.

"I'm Cecil." He reached out his hand, and she extended her own. "Cecil Jenkins."

The second they touched, a bolt of electricity coursed through her entire body, and everything turned bright white. The flash blinded her, then faded as suddenly as it had come. When it went away, Evelyn wasn't in the street anymore. She was in an office building. And it looked different from the office buildings she was used to in 1922. She couldn't quite put her finger on it until she looked out of a long, rectangular window where a bevy of flags flapped proudly in the wind. She finally put it all together. She was inside the UN building. In her other timeline.

Aside from the shock of suddenly being thrust back into the life she previously believed she'd lost all access to, her body was light and almost floating. It was as if she wasn't truly there. As she tried to decipher the situation, movement nearby grabbed her attention.

Someone was sitting in an office chair, facing the window with the flags. Her heart jumped into her throat. She would recognize that head of hair anywhere. Before she could get closer, she started fading away from this place, no matter how desperately her heart yearned to stay. He turned in his chair to reach for a pen, and Evelyn saw his face, lit up by the blue light of the computer screen in front of him. It was Will, and he was everything she'd been dreaming of for the past three years.

She opened her mouth to say something to him, but as she did, she saw the glaring flash of light again. Before she knew it, she was back on the sidewalk in 1922 with Cecil Jenkins.

Jenkins?

Evelyn's heart was racing a mile a minute.

"Are you quite all right?" Cecil's voice jostled her back into reality. "You've gone a bit pale. Are you feeling well?"

"I'm fine," Evelyn assured him. "Thank you."

"I must be going, I'm afraid." Cecil pointed in the direction he had been walking.

"Yes, of course. I didn't mean to keep you." Evelyn desperately wanted to touch his hand again so she could go back to Will.

"Well, I suppose next time you see me, you'll know where we met. Right here!" Cecil grinned at his own joke. "Good day, Evelyn."

Evelyn laughed slightly and said her goodbyes, her mind eight and a half decades away. As she watched Cecil disappear down the block, her head swirled with the possibilities that came with the revelation she'd just had. Cecil was the key to seeing Will again. And she had every intention of doing exactly that. She simply had to figure out how.

After a hasty walk from the bank, Evelyn burst through the door of her apartment and threw her bag down on the couch on her way into the bedroom. She flung open her closet door and scanned a stack of shoe boxes she'd lined up neatly along the left wall. She spotted the box she was looking for and carefully pulled it out from the pile. She opened it and removed a pair of white canvas heels with black patent trim, setting them aside, then lifted the layer of tissue paper at the bottom of the box and retrieved her hidden journal. She hadn't written any real entries since her dreams had stopped, but this book was where she'd recorded every sighting of who she now knew was Cecil Jenkins.

Opening the journal, Evelyn grabbed a pen from her nightstand, sat down on the edge of her bed, and began writing furiously.

Dear Journal,

I finally talked to him. The man who looks like Will. His name is Cecil Jenkins! He must be related to Will. Perhaps his grandfather or great-grandfather? When I touched his hand, I went blind momentarily and then had the strangest, most wonderful experience. I was in Will's office. In 2006. And I saw him. I saw his face!

It was as beautiful as I remembered it. Those verdant green eyes with the unruly hair that never stops falling into them. His strong cheekbones. The gentle curve of his lips. I fell in love with him all over again.

He didn't see me. I tried to talk to him, but I was back here in 1922 before I could say anything, and I have no idea if I can ever get back to 2006.

I have to find Cecil and touch his hand again. I have to get back to Will.

Evelyn froze when she heard Thomas's keys jingling outside the apartment door. He was a frequent visitor to the building, and she'd instructed Edward, the elevator attendant and her good friend, to let Thomas up anytime. Jolting herself to action, she slammed the journal shut, stuffing it back into the shoebox and sliding the stack of boxes back into the closet as quickly as she could. The black-and-white shoes were still on the carpet in front of the closet, but she could explain those away easily enough. She had barely closed the closet door when Thomas walked into the apartment. She tried to calm her breathing as she greeted him in the living room.

"How was your day?" she asked, hoping he wouldn't notice anything amiss.

"Busy!" He took off his hat and coat and placed them on the sofa. "I'm starved. Are you ready to go to dinner?"

"Yes, I just need five minutes to freshen up."

"You look perfectly fresh to me." He winked at her.

"Are you flirting with me, Mr. Allen?"

He laughed as she exited the room. His attempt at light-heartedness touched her. They rarely bantered back and forth like they used to, and she was relieved he hadn't noticed how nervous she was. Evelyn hurried to get ready for their date. She decided to wear the black-and-white shoes since they were already out. She used to wear them to work at the law office. She'd forgotten how much she liked them.

Dinner was pleasant, in spite of Thomas being slightly distracted. She assumed he was thinking about work again. It was already difficult to stay fully present with him given everything that happened to her that day, and with him also off in another world, they may as well have been dining separately. She hated keeping secrets from Thomas and briefly considered telling him about the flash forward. After all, he'd been instrumental in figuring out her time-traveling dreams back in 1919 and surely would be again if she asked for his help now. But if he found out she'd gone to 2006, it could destroy everything they'd built and risk her only opportunity to ever see Will again.

Evelyn wasn't prepared to take that chance.

Chapter 6
2006

Will sat waiting for Cammie outside a coffee shop near work. They hadn't spoken since their kiss, but he didn't want to lose her as a friend, so he'd sent her a text message asking her if she wanted to meet him and talk.

Will wasn't completely sure how he felt about the kiss. He'd been a little drunk when it happened, but he clearly remembered liking it. He had no idea exactly what Cammie thought, but her silence over the past few days was a pretty strong hint that she was, at the very least, feeling awkward. He figured it meant she wasn't interested in him romantically, which was fine. His main concern was salvaging their friendship. He didn't have many people he could talk to or spend time with these days, and he wasn't prepared to lose anyone else. He ordered her a coffee while he waited for her to arrive.

A few minutes later, Cammie walked in and sat down without giving him a hug like she usually did. This was worse than he thought.

"Hey." The discomfort was evident in her voice and the tension in her shoulders. "Sorry I'm late."

"Hey, no problem at all. Here, I got you some coffee." He slid the cup across the table, offering a modern-day olive branch and hoping the gesture would help smooth things over a little.

"Thanks." She took the cup in her hands. Her jaw clenched tightly, and Will immediately regretted causing her so much stress.

"I'm really sorry about what happened the other night," he began bluntly. "I had a few drinks, and I don't know what I was thinking. I shouldn't have kissed you."

She took a sip from her cup and swallowed. "I'm the one who kissed you."

Will opened his mouth to respond but couldn't seem to form the words. It had all happened fast, and he'd been drinking a bit, but he assumed he'd been the one making the bad decisions, not Cammie.

"I'm not sure what came over me," she continued. "We were just talking about Evelyn, and it was as if you were the one person in the world who understood exactly how I felt." The words tumbled out, her nerves clearly shot. "I guess I misread the situation. I'm so sorry, Will."

"Cammie, don't apologize. Please." He reached forward and moved to place his hand on hers atop the table but retracted it on second thought. "We've both been through hell. It's understandable that we'd have moments of weakness. But you're the only person in this world who cares if I live or die right now. Your friendship is important to me. I don't want to lose you."

She looked down at her coffee cup and back up slowly, finally meeting his eyes. "The problem is, I haven't been able to stop thinking about that kiss since it happened."

"Me neither," he admitted. "I really hope we can move past this and still be friends."

"No, you don't get it." She put her hands over her face and sighed deeply before explaining. "I can't stop thinking about it because I liked it."

Will leaned back in his seat, unsure of what his next move should be. He'd never even considered the possibility that Cammie had enjoyed the kiss. He needed some time to process the twist in this story.

"Ugh, I knew it. I've screwed everything up. I'm such an idiot!" Cammie looked at the ceiling, exasperated.

"No! No, you haven't." He straightened back up. "It's just . . . not what I was expecting you to say."

"I know it's totally disrespectful of your relationship with Evelyn, and I never meant to—"

He reached for her hands again, this time taking them in his own. "Stop, it's okay. We're okay."

She immediately relaxed her shoulders and looked at him, her misty eyes wide as she let him hold her hands. "Really?"

"Of course," Will said. "Cammie, it's been three years since Evelyn died, and almost a year since I lost my mom. That kiss was the first time I've felt alive since before any of it happened."

She took her hands back and gathered her hair into a ponytail at the nape of her neck, letting it go after a few seconds. Will was painfully aware that she was wrestling internally with so many complicated facets of their situation and completely tongue-tied.

He reached into his pocket and pulled out a tattered piece of folded note paper. Cammie recognized it immediately. She had a letter from Evelyn on the exact same stationery. She tried not to cry as Will carefully unfolded the now-delicate correspondence and handed it to her. "Read this."

He sat silently, sipping his coffee as Cammie read the letter Evelyn had penned to the love of her life before she'd left him forever.

"*When I'm gone, I want you to take our love and spread it. With someone new.*" Cammie read out loud, tears now streaming down her cheeks. "You really think she was including her best friend in that pool of potential someones?"

"I think she loved and respected you more than anyone else, and she would want you to be happy, just like she wanted me to be happy. I'm not saying we should dive headfirst into a relationship, but I am saying if you want to explore the idea, slowly, together, I don't think there's anything wrong with that. If it went anywhere, I'd like to believe Evelyn would give us her blessing. And you shouldn't beat yourself up over it."

"Can I think about it?"

"You don't even have to give me an answer. Ever. We can just go back to being friends and forget this ever happened if that's what you want." He meant it. He wasn't trying to pressure her into anything, and he was perfectly willing to keep her in his life simply as the supportive, fun friend she'd always been.

"Okay," Cammie whispered. "Thank you."

Will was eager to change the subject and give Cammie a clean exit from their tense conversation. "Can I tell you something crazy that happened to me last night at work?"

"Um, sure." She cocked her head, curious about where this was going.

"So, I was all alone in the office late yesterday," he began. "And I got this weird feeling, like I wasn't really alone, like someone was standing right next to me. I mean I know obviously no one was there."

Cammie raised her eyebrows. "You know I don't like ghost stories, right?"

Will laughed quietly. "I don't either, but this didn't feel scary. For a second I wondered if it was my mom, and I know this sounds weird, but in my gut I know it wasn't." He stopped to gauge her reaction.

She stared at him without blinking, piecing together what he was getting at. "Wait, so you're telling me you think Evelyn's ghost visited you at work?"

"Well, when you say it like that, you make me sound like a lunatic. And I don't know if it was a ghost, necessarily, but . . . it felt like her. I don't know how to explain it."

Cammie stood up and walked around the table to him, bending down to hug him from behind. "I don't believe in that kind of stuff," she said softly into his ear as she squeezed him. "But I really want you to be right. I want to believe she's looking out for us, too."

Chapter 7

1922

It was early, and Evelyn wasn't even sure Holstead would be up yet, but she couldn't wait another second to talk to him about her strange experience visiting Will in 2006. She had not only confirmed that there was more to her dreams and time traveling than they'd previously thought but also discovered a way she could see Will again, and she needed to know more.

She ran up the steps and rapped on Holstead's front door, hoping she wasn't too early. Mrs. Brooks answered, surprised to see Evelyn. "Oh, I thought you were the milkman!" She ushered Evelyn inside. "Are you all right, dear? Why the early visit?"

"Mrs. Brooks, I'm so sorry to bother you and the doctor so early in the morning, but I have something I urgently need to discuss with him. Is he up?"

"He's just gotten out of bed. Why don't I make you some tea while you wait for him to dress?"

Evelyn politely agreed and waited in the small sitting room sipping her tea while she waited for Holstead. All she could think about was how to get back to Will. To have the chance to talk to him. To touch him again. She had so much she still wanted to say. Every second spent waiting for Holstead to appear was like torture.

Shortly, Holstead entered the room, beaming at Evelyn in spite of the early hour at which she'd arrived. "Up with the sparrows today, are we?"

"I'm sorry. I couldn't sleep. Something big has happened."

Holstead nodded in understanding and closed the doors to the sitting room before he sat across from her. "Tell me everything."

Evelyn recounted to Holstead her meeting with Cecil and how shaking his hand had somehow propelled her into her old timeline where she'd seen Will. Holstead listened intently, too shocked to interrupt. When she finished speaking, he sat back in his chair and ran his hands over his beard, deep in thought. It was a few moments before he finally spoke. "I need to go to Fletch's."

Chapter 8

1922

Later that day, Evelyn paced anxiously in her living room, imagining what Holstead might be learning about her flashes at that very minute. It aggravated her that she couldn't do anything but wait while he visited Fletcher's widow in a bid to search his office for anything that might help Evelyn solve her newest mystery. Eager to pass the time, she retrieved her journal from its closet hiding spot and sat down at the dining room table to write.

Dear Journal,

I'm going crazy waiting to hear back from Dr. Holstead. It's only been a few hours since I left his house, but it feels like days, and I wish there was something I could do in the meantime to find more answers. Seeing Will for those few seconds the other day was like heaven, and I know it's wrong, but I can't shake how badly I want to see him again. Even if it's just for another few moments. I can't put my finger on it, but he looked different, somehow. Something's changed. I have to know what's happened. It's consuming my thoughts! If only I could flash forward again.

Evelyn put down her pen and slammed the journal shut. Seeing Cecil again was the one thing she *could* do while she waited for Holstead to find more information about the flashes. She hastily stuffed the journal under a throw pillow on the sofa, making a mental note to put it away properly later, and hurried out of the apartment toward the bank where she'd seen Cecil a couple of days before. It was about the same time of day, and he would be leaving work again soon. She pretended to be reading a newspaper while she waited near the bank, but her eyes were trained on every person who exited the impressive building and came down its stone steps.

Finally, she saw the figure that made her stomach flip even though she knew he wasn't Will. The resemblance was enough to trick Evelyn's heart into fluttering as though he were. She made her way quickly toward the sidewalk at the bottom of the bank's massive staircase, carefully timing her approach so that she and Cecil would meet again. The cold air must have surprised him, because he buttoned his long coat as he came down the stairs, and didn't see Evelyn. He bumped straight into her as he stepped onto the sidewalk, nearly toppling her. Evelyn grabbed his forearm to steady herself, and once again, that single touch from Cecil propelled her eighty-four years into the future, where she found herself on the sidewalk in 2006 New York.

It had been a few years since she'd been in the New York City streets of the next millennium, but she quickly got her bearings. She was near Lenox Hill Hospital, where Cammie had been working before Evelyn passed. There was no way to know whether Cammie was still there. She could be at any hospital anywhere in the country by now. Evelyn swallowed hard as the memory of her best friend caused her throat to swell with emotion. She had to focus and figure out where Will was. Carefully scanning the sidewalks around her, Evelyn gasped, and her breath became stuck in her chest at the sight of him seated at a table outside a coffee shop. A woman was embracing him from behind, bent over, whispering in his ear. He turned his head and smiled at her. From her vantage point, Evelyn couldn't tell whether they were kissing, but it certainly looked like they were. The woman lifted her head, and Evelyn finally got a chance to see her face.

"Cammie?!"

In another momentary bright flash, Evelyn was out of 2006 and back outside the bank with Cecil in 1922. He had backed up a bit and her hand had fallen off his arm, for which she was strangely grateful. She would rather never have seen what she'd just witnessed. Her best friend and the love of her life were dating. She felt nauseous.

"I'm sorry, I wasn't paying attention to where I was going. Forgive me. Long day at the bank." Cecil looked up and instantly recognized Evelyn. "Ah! We meet again!" He beamed, blissfully unaware of her inner turmoil.

She had to pull herself together quickly. She forced a smile. "Yes! What are the chances?"

"Well, I should be going," Cecil said, "but I suppose I'll run into you again here at this rate! Hopefully with less force next time." The twinkle in his eye when he made a joke was exactly the same as the one in

Will's. Jealousy and pain coursed through Evelyn's veins as she tried to accept that Will's eyes were twinkling for Cammie at that very moment.

"Until next time." Cecil tipped his hat and walked away.

Evelyn stood rooted to the spot for a few moments, unsure how to proceed with the agonizing new information she now had. After a few seconds spent deep in thought, she marched across the street, narrowly missing a passing car, and walked as fast as she could to Holstead's house. Every hour since she'd seen him earlier that day was endless, and she couldn't wait any longer to learn what he'd found at Fletch's house.

Finally sitting across from Holstead in his office, Evelyn was still struggling to hide the anger and hurt that had overtaken her mind and body since the flash forward. She hadn't told Holstead about seeing Cecil again, but he was the only person who could help her decipher the flashes and what they meant. Aside from wanting to know more about Will and Cammie, it was imperative that she uncover as much information as she could about her abilities and how they might affect her in the future. She wanted to be as honest with Thomas as she could about the dreams and everything associated with them, but she was still trying to make sense of everything she'd learned on her own and wasn't sure how she'd even begin to explain anything to him yet. She watched impatiently as Holstead shuffled through the files and opened them to the pages he wanted her to see.

"What I am about to show you is information that I myself have just learned," Holstead told her firmly. "I had walked away from the dreamer project by the time Fletch studied any of what's in these files." He paused to find the right words to warn Evelyn about the emotional dangers of pursuing the flashes. "You need to remember that this is untested research. I don't want you to get your hopes up about what we—what *you* can do with this information."

Evelyn nodded in agreement.

Holstead continued, "Before he got sick, Fletch was in the early stages of studying whether dreamers who had lost one of their timelines might be able to restart the dreams or somehow go back to their other lives again."

"Like my flashes?"

"Wasn't it just the one?" Holstead cocked his head.

"I . . . might have bumped into Cecil Jenkins again this afternoon." She clasped her hands in her lap and stared at them.

"I see." He sighed and shook his head in mock defeat before continuing. "Fletch found what you and I already know: that touching a person with a strong physical connection to someone in the other timeline has the power to send dreamers back into their other lives. According to these files, Fletch knew a bit more about the flashes before he died. He and another dreamer had discovered the ability to bounce between timelines even after the dreams had ended. The same way you went to 2006."

Evelyn's mind was racing. "So what else did Fletcher find out about the flashes?"

"That's the real question, isn't it?" Holstead replied. "These files hint at some additional research that Fletch may have wanted . . . kept hidden."

"Hidden?" Evelyn's brow furrowed in confusion.

Holstead sat back in his chair. "The book Fletcher published about the dreamer research wasn't exactly met with a positive response from the medical community," he said wistfully. "I had a feeling that's how it was going to go. It's part of the reason I walked away before it was written."

"Was it the time travel part that put them off?"

"Absolutely. The science of dreams and sleep had only just begun to be studied, and the mere suggestion that dreams might be propelling people into alternate timelines was, understandably, a bit much for most doctors and medical officials to swallow. I imagine Fletch wanted the files hidden away so he could never be posthumously ridiculed for his research."

"I suppose it's too much for anyone to take in, really." Evelyn scoffed. "Unless you're close to a dreamer, it sounds daft, doesn't it? Even when I was in 2003, time travel was still just an idea. A concept in movies and books. I chalked up my own traveling to dreams until I met you."

Holstead chuckled. "It's too bad Fletch never got to meet you." After a few seconds of silence, he added, "I need to get back into his office and find the additional files."

"How do you know there are more files in his office?"

Holstead smiled and held up a small piece of paper with some words scrawled on it. "Fletch told me."

Chapter 9
2006

The flags of the world were flapping hard in the chill wind as Will left the UN building after work. His stomach was in knots while he rode the subway to Cammie's apartment, where he was scheduled to pick her up for their first official date.

He had been wrestling with himself all day over whether going out with Evelyn's best friend was a good idea, but he also hadn't looked forward to an evening this much in a long time. Will vowed he would allow himself to lean into the date with Cammie and try to enjoy the night as much as possible without overthinking it. They'd agreed to take things slowly. Cammie was missing Evelyn just as much as he was. He walked up to her building and buzzed her apartment to let her know he was outside. While he waited for her to come down, he put his hand in his pocket and felt the letter he always carried with him. It had been another inner battle with himself over whether to bring it on this date, but he wasn't sure he was ready to leave home without it yet. He closed his eyes and whispered out loud, "Please be okay with this, Evelyn."

Just as he opened his eyes, Cammie appeared. Will had to remind himself to view her as a date, not as a friend. She looked beautiful. She was dressed in dark denim jeans with wedge heels and a light blue sweater layered over a white tank top. Her chestnut brown hair was pulled into a messy bun on top of her head.

"Oh look, it's my date!" She laughed as she approached him. "That's so weird to say, isn't it?"

Will grinned and greeted her with a hug. "A little."

"So, where to?"

"Dinner?"

"Honestly, I know it sounds strange, but I'm a little nervous." She glanced away. "Let's go get one quick drink before dinner to calm my nerves."

Will was feeling nervous himself. "I'm glad you said it first. I know a place." They walked a couple of blocks making stiff small talk until Will stopped and opened the door for her.

It was dark inside the Irish pub. A single flameless candle lit the small booth Will and Cammie were in as they waited for their drinks.

"I know we aren't supposed to talk about it, but I can tell something's off. Are you sure you're okay with this?" Cammie asked. "We don't have to drink if that's what's bothering you."

Will glanced up at her. She'd always been a straight shooter, and though it often caught people off guard, he appreciated that she never left anyone guessing. "No, the drinks aren't the problem. I guess I'm feeling guilty, which I know is stupid, but—"

"It's not stupid," Cammie interjected. "I do, too." A server appeared and placed their drinks on the table, along with a basket of pub chips. They thanked her before Cammie continued. "You know, Evelyn asked me to take care of you."

Will froze in the middle of reaching for a chip. "What do you mean?" he asked, his face scrunched in confusion.

"In her letter to me before she died. She asked me to make sure you were okay. That you were happy. Moving on."

He leaned back in his seat, thoughtful as he took a slow sip of his drink. "Do you think this is what she had in mind?"

"I think it's like you said: she'd want us to explore it if we thought it would bring us happiness," Cammie stated matter-of-factly. "It's not the usual 'don't date the ex' situation, you know? It's not like I'm dating my best friend's ex in front of her face. We'd obviously never even consider it if she were still here."

"True," Will admitted. He needed to change the subject before the night started off on the wrong note and they couldn't recover. "You look really pretty tonight, by the way."

She beamed at him from across the table. "Now *that's* how a date talks." She raised her glass. "To finding happiness, even if it feels weird." She laughed.

"To happiness." He clinked his glass against hers.

An hour later, the two were still seated in the booth at the pub. They'd decided to stay and chat over appetizers. Will was surprised at how easy it was to open up to Cammie. He hadn't sat with a woman and had such an in-depth conversation since Evelyn. It was refreshing. For the first time in months, he felt a glimmer of his old self kindling within. He allowed himself to relax and enjoy something for once as he and Cammie

shared dessert.

Chapter 10

1922

Evelyn walked home from Doctor Holstead's house. The fresh air helped clear her head as she reeled from everything she'd seen and heard that afternoon. She couldn't get the image of Will and Cammie kissing out of her head, and every time it appeared, a pain filled her chest and she had to fight back tears.

Will and Cammie weren't doing anything wrong. At least that's what she tried to tell herself. It had been years since she'd left their lives, and though she was currently regretting it, she had told Will in no uncertain terms that she wanted him to move on and find happiness after she was gone. She'd just never imagined it would be with her best friend. Evelyn couldn't wait to be in the privacy of her apartment. She needed to cry or scream or maybe throw something to release the abundance of emotions that were boiling inside her.

She kept her composure as she greeted Edward and stepped into the elevator.

"Good evening, Miss Moore." He smiled. "Fun plans with Mr. Allen this evening?"

"Not that I'm aware of," she answered, suddenly nervous she'd forgotten something important.

"I'm sorry, I just assumed. I let him in a few minutes ago. I thought he was picking you up."

Evelyn couldn't recall having plans with Thomas that evening, but he often stopped by on his way home from work to see her and have dinner together. She thanked Edward and headed for her apartment. The timing of Thomas's visit wasn't ideal, but she would have to get through it.

She unlocked the door and went in. Thomas was sitting on the couch in the living room exactly where she usually found him when he arrived before she got home.

"You beat me here!" she exclaimed as she hung up her coat and hat. "I thought you'd have another late night at the office."

He didn't reply. Evelyn walked into the living room, concerned. Something was wrong. There was no happy hello, and he wasn't standing up to greet her with a warm hug like he usually did. When she got closer, the color drained from Evelyn's face as she caught sight of her journal on the coffee table in front of him, open to her last entry from that morning.

"We need to talk." He leaned back and folded his arms across his chest, strangely calm.

She couldn't think of a single thing to say that would help, so she silently sat beside him on the couch and closed the journal. "I'm sorry, Thomas." She could barely get the words out.

"Why didn't you tell me?"

"I . . . I didn't want to ruin everything. I needed to know if the dreams were over before I told you." She looked deeply into his eyes, hoping he would understand.

"Of all the people in the world, you didn't think you could come to me with this?" He smacked the back of his hand against her journal. "Why are you keeping things from me? Don't you trust me?"

"Of course I trust you!" She clutched his arm as she pleaded. "I didn't know what I was seeing when I saw the doppelgänger. I thought I was going insane!"

He took a deep breath inward, trying to gain his composure. "You saw Will in his timeline. And you didn't tell me."

It was like a punch to the gut. Thomas had always been a bit jealous when it came to Will, and she could see how the new developments would upset him. She had to tell him about what she'd learned—and seen—earlier that day. She was dreading his reaction. They'd been on a relatively good streak lately, after a long few weeks of squabbling. The last thing she wanted was to disrupt their relationship, but he could never fully understand how badly she needed to find answers about the flashes.

"I know you're hurt." She reached for his hand, but he pulled away before she could touch it. The simple gesture said more than his words could, and her heart broke a little. "I just wanted to find out what it meant. See if it was really all over."

His gaze was locked on the closed journal. "As long as you feel like *that* about someone else, it'll never be over, Evelyn."

She glanced at the journal and tried to remember everything she'd written that morning.

"Let me refresh your memory," Thomas quipped. "Seeing Will's face was 'like heaven' and you simply *must* see him again. Does that sound familiar?"

She dug her fingertips into her palms as she tried to think of what to say that could make it better. The truth was, he was right. Seeing Will had been like heaven. And she did want to see him again. Of course, she couldn't say that to her fiancé.

"Thomas, you know I love you—"

"Let me just stop you right there." His eyes bore holes into her own as he spoke. "I love you, too, but I've done all this before. I've already fought against an invisible man from the future for your love once. I don't know if I can do it again, Evelyn."

"What are you saying?" She was afraid to hear the answer.

"I can't spend the rest of my life coming in second to someone I'll never meet. As much as I try to understand, it's impossible to share you with anyone, let alone a ghost."

"Are you calling off the engagement?" she whispered.

"That's up to you. I'm asking you to make a choice."

Evelyn's heart skipped a beat, anticipating the impossible ultimatum Thomas was about to issue. She swallowed hard and stared at him in silence as he continued.

"I know you're a dreamer, and I wish I could accept everything that comes with it, but I can't. I'm sorry, I thought I could handle it, but maybe I'm not a strong enough person, or maybe I'm just not the right one for you. I don't want to share my wife with someone else, even if it's just the memory of them that's coming between us. I want to marry you more than anything, Evelyn, but I need you to decide: either we part ways and you chase the answers about the flashes and keep visiting Will, or be with me once and for all and let's just live our lives together. No more dreamer stuff."

She stared at him, dumbfounded. It was an impossible choice, and he knew it. "I don't know what to say to that."

Thomas stood and walked around the coffee table toward the front door.

"Where are you going?" Evelyn jumped up from the sofa and walked after him, desperate for more time to talk and smooth things over.

"Let me know when you've made your decision."

He closed the door behind him and left her alone, shaking. Evelyn slid her back down the door until she was on the floor, sobbing out every emotion she'd been bottling up that day. She was heartbroken over her fractured relationship, confused about Will and Cammie, and furious that her dreams were once again disrupting her reality.

A few minutes later, she sat up straight, caught her breath, and wiped the tears away from her eyes. There was only one thing to do.

Chapter 11

1922

The next day, Evelyn made her way to Holstead's house again. Instead of knocking before he woke up this time, she sat outside and waited. After forty-five minutes by Evelyn's best estimation, the front door finally opened, and the doctor appeared. He jumped, startled to see her on his doorstep first thing in the morning.

"Evelyn! What are you doing here?"

She stood and faced him. "I'm coming with you to Fletch's."

Moments later, the two were huddled in a taxi on the way to the Fletcher residence. In an attempt to quell her own anxiety, Evelyn tried to make conversation.

"What is Doctor Fletcher's wife like?"

Holstead grinned. "Mariah is a wonderful woman. She's always been kind and welcoming. I'm sure you'll like her very much."

"Did you stay in touch with her after he passed?"

"Going to find those research files in his office the other day was our first meeting in many years."

A tinge of guilt hit Evelyn as she realized she'd prompted what may have been an uncomfortable reunion. "I'm sorry. I didn't mean to cause any awkwardness."

"Actually, it was very nice catching up with Mariah," Holstead assured her. "I've been hemming and hawing over paying her a visit for years. This was the push I needed to actually do it. She seemed genuinely happy to see me. I don't think she's gotten out much since Fletch passed."

Evelyn relaxed a bit, relieved. She took a few seconds to contemplate whether she should ask the question that had been burning in the back of her mind since she'd met Holstead. "May I ask, what happened between you and Doctor Fletcher that made you stop talking?"

Holstead shifted in his seat and sighed before he answered. "Fletcher was always more willing to push the boundaries when it came to our studies. We had many disagreements over the years about how far we could push the dreamers before the studies became unethical."

Evelyn said nothing, prompting Holstead to go on.

"Some of the dreamers were showing signs of mental and physical fatigue. I wanted to stop and publish what we'd already discovered. It was enough to fill a book, and it was my opinion that we could do so without further harming any dreamers. One day Fletch proposed an experiment I was most uncomfortable with, and he made it clear he would proceed with or without my consent. He was going to publish his findings either way and said I could stay and be part of what he whole-heartedly believed would be groundbreaking research, or I could leave and he'd go on without me. After quite a row, it was clear I wasn't going to change his mind, so I left. And I never went back."

"And you never spoke to him again?"

Holstead gazed sadly at the floor of the cab. "No."

Evelyn could sense the regret in his voice. She patted his hand softly. "If it's any consolation, I'm sure you were right."

The taxi soon dropped Evelyn and Holstead off outside the Fletchers' residence, and the two headed up the steps to the front door. Holstead knocked. As they waited for an answer, he finally asked Evelyn the obvious question.

"What made you decide to come and see me again this morning?"

She lowered her eyes. "Thomas gave me no choice."

Before he could respond, the door opened. Mariah Fletcher beamed when she saw Holstead again. "Back so soon!" She stepped aside so he could enter.

"I hope you don't mind, but I've brought a friend along today." Holstead went inside as he gestured at Evelyn behind him. "Mrs. Mariah Fletcher, this is Evelyn Moore."

Mrs. Fletcher's head snapped up at the mention of Evelyn's name. She looked at Evelyn, squinting, seemingly thrown by Holstead's introduction. "A pleasure to meet you," she finally said, reaching her hand out to Evelyn. "Please, come in."

Evelyn thought Mariah's reaction was a little strange but chalked it up to the fact that she'd been surprised with a guest.

Holstead fibbed. "Evelyn is assisting me with some errands today." They'd agreed not to tell Mariah that Evelyn was a dreamer.

"Of course." Mrs. Fletcher took their coats. "I'm sorry, I don't get many visitors these days."

"I hope it's not a bother that we're here," Evelyn said.

"Not at all!" Mariah smiled. Her face was kind, but sadness lurked behind her eyes. Evelyn guessed that had to do with the loss of her husband.

"I'm afraid I may have missed some files when I was here the other day," Holstead explained. "I was wondering if I could get another look around the office?"

"Yes, of course. I'll show you in." Mariah led them down the hall and into Fletcher's study. It was spacious and tidy. The opposite of Holstead's, Evelyn noticed with amusement.

"I'll make some tea while you look for your files." Mariah quickly turned and disappeared back down the hall. Evelyn gazed around the large office, wondering where to begin the search. Holstead was already opening drawers and cabinets hunting for the secret papers. Evelyn followed suit, searching the bookshelves for anything that might be helpful. She quickly became frustrated with aimlessly searching.

"What exactly did the note from Fletcher say?"

"What note?" Holstead replied, his head deep in a filing cabinet.

"The note that told you there was more research in this office for you to find."

"Ah." Holstead straightened up and took the small piece of paper from his pocket. He read it aloud.

"Walter, I knew you'd be back for more. If you're reading this, then you'll need the additional hidden files in my office. They will paint a much clearer picture of what you're looking for. Fletch."

Evelyn sighed. The note was rather unhelpful. She looked around the room, lost in thought. She scanned the shelves, the desktop, the walls. Suddenly, her eyes came to rest on something that made her gasp. She straightened up and walked quickly toward a painting hung across the room. It was a framed oil on canvas depicting a herd of horses grazing in a field. Evelyn touched the upper corner of the frame. She tugged on it gently, and it pulled away from the wall, the far edge on hinges. Behind it, a safe was built carefully into the wall. "I found it!" she announced proudly. Holstead whooped out loud and came over to look at the safe. It was secured by a combination lock that used a four-digit code.

"What could it be?" Holstead wondered aloud, gently fiddling with the combination. He tried a few numbers that Fletcher might have used to safeguard secret research, but none of them opened the lock. He guessed at several more combinations in vain. They could be there all day if they kept it up, so Evelyn sprang into action.

"You keep trying to open the safe. I'm going to see if Mrs. Fletcher needs any help with the tea." She walked out of the room and tiptoed down the hall back toward the front door, unsure which way to go to find the kitchen. When she passed a room with its door ajar, she stopped. Someone was crying softly. Evelyn peeked through the small gap in the doorway. Mariah was in a small sitting room, dabbing her eyes with a handkerchief.

Evelyn knocked gently on the door. "Mrs. Fletcher? Are you all right?" She pushed the door open slightly and stepped into the room. The older woman looked up at her, surprised, and tried to hide that she'd been crying, straightening her hair and wiping the watery evidence from her cheeks.

"This is embarrassing, I'm so sorry." She laughed awkwardly as she covered her face with her hands.

Evelyn sat down next to her. "Please, don't apologize. Is there anything I can do?"

"Oh, no." Mariah was still trying to catch her breath fully. "I suppose seeing Walter—Doctor Holstead—after all these years is just bringing back a lot of memories of my husband."

"I can't imagine how hard that must be. I'm so sorry." Evelyn sat beside her, and Mariah's expression went from sad to the hint of a smile. "You're very kind. This isn't exactly the ideal first meeting, is it?" She faked another faint chuckle.

"It's fine, really," Evelyn insisted. "I wish there was something I could do to help."

"It's nice just to have company, actually." Mariah looked around the room. "Living alone in this giant house all these years has been so quiet and dull."

"Well, if it's any help, I'd be happy to come around now and then. We can chat. Get to know each other." Evelyn meant it. She felt sorry for Mrs. Fletcher. She also acknowledged it was her fault Mariah was upset. If it wasn't for Evelyn, Holstead would have never come here and drummed up memories of Mariah's husband. Offering her friendship was the least Evelyn could do in return for the answers Mariah would hopefully help her find.

Mariah looked as though she was about to burst into tears again, only this time out of what Evelyn read as gratitude. "That would be nice," Mariah choked out as she smiled. "I would like that very much."

Just then, the kettle whistled loudly from the kitchen.

Evelyn stood. "Shall I help you with the tea?"

"Thank you." They both knew Mariah wasn't thanking her for helping in the kitchen.

"You're welcome. Lead the way!"

Mariah showed Evelyn to the kitchen. As they prepared a tray of tea, Evelyn turned her attention back to the real reason she'd come out of the office in the first place. "Mrs. Fletcher, your husband pointed Doctor Holstead to some files he's kept hidden in a safe in his office. We found the safe, but there was nothing in his note about how to open it. Do you know what the combination might be?"

Mrs. Fletcher paused, arranging the cookies on a plate, and looked at Evelyn. "I think I might." She grinned slyly, a little glint in her eye.

A few minutes later, the two women entered the office, where Holstead had moved on from trying to guess the combination and was combing through some books instead. He put the book down when they came in.

"How did you know I was starved? Thank you!" He walked over to the desk where Evelyn had placed the tea tray. As he poured himself a cup, Mrs. Fletcher approached the safe with trepidation. When she got to the painting, still opened up revealing the safe behind it, she lifted her hand and twisted the four dials. The lock clicked open.

"Ah-ha!" Holstead exclaimed, victorious. "Thank you, Mariah!" He abandoned his cup on the desk and rushed over to retrieve the contents of the safe.

Mrs. Fletcher nodded as Holstead pulled out another bundle of research papers wrapped in brown paper and string, just like the last batch. He pulled a small piece of white note paper from the string and read it aloud. "*You got the picture.*"

The three shared a laugh. "Fletch always was the master of a good pun." Holstead paused, glanced at the safe, then back at Mariah. "What was the combination, after all that?"

Mariah smiled mischievously. "That's a story for another day."

Holstead took one last sip from his teacup and picked up the files from the desk. "We should be going, Mariah. We've kept you long enough."

Mrs. Fletcher took the files from his hands and placed them back on the desktop. She grinned and shook her head at her old friend. "You haven't changed a bit. Always rushing off to find the next answer. Let's finish our tea first."

Chapter 12
2006

The morning after his date with Cammie, Will arrived at work ten minutes early, causing Jamie to do a double take. Will hadn't been early to work in months. Recently, he'd barely even made it on time most days.

"You have a good night?" Jamie asked, poking his head into Will's office.

"I did, actually." Will grinned back at his boss. "Hoping to make it a regular thing."

"Well, if it gets you in here early, I'm all for . . . whatever it is!" Jamie chuckled as he disappeared back into his own office.

Will flew through his inbox and even managed to knock out a couple of projects he'd been putting off for weeks. It was the most productive day he'd had in a while, and he credited his night with Cammie for his uptick in motivation. In spite of their reservations, they'd actually hit it off better than he expected, and Will had to admit he'd woken up happy for the first time in a long time. When his lunch break rolled around, he stayed in the building and ate in the cafeteria. As he munched on a sandwich, he sent Cammie a text message.

What are you doing tonight?

He hoped it wasn't too much or too soon.

That night, Cammie knocked on Will's apartment door at eight o'clock on the dot. Will greeted her with a warm hug and a peck on the lips. To his relief, she didn't seem fazed. They'd shared a few brief kisses at the pub the night before, so it wasn't out of the blue.

"I didn't think our second date would be this soon," she said as she walked in.

"I didn't either." He took her jacket and hung it in the coat closet. "I just didn't have anything planned tonight, and last night went so well. I figured, why not?"

As they entered his living room, a loud clap of thunder shook the entire building, making them both jump. Cammie giggled at their reaction over what was obviously just a storm.

Will peeked through the curtains. It was pouring rain. "Well I did have tickets to a free concert in the park, but I guess that's not happening. What's plan B?"

"I don't know." Cammie joined him at the window. "Wow, it's really coming down out there."

"We could order in?"

"Will you watch *American Idol* reruns with me?" She raised her eyebrows hopefully. "I was working nights when it aired and I didn't get to watch."

"Do I have to promise not to cringe the whole time?"

"You get three visible cringes, and the rest have to be internal."

"You drive a hard bargain, but I accept." They laughed as he reached out his hand to shake on their agreement.

"Since I'm forcing you to sit through *Idol*, you get to pick where we order from," she acquiesced.

"Firm, but fair. I like it." He was glad he'd invited her over.

An hour later, they were sitting cross-legged at his coffee table, watching *Idol* hopefuls sing their hearts out and enjoying dinner from the taqueria down the street. Will had used up his three cringes before the first commercial break, and a particularly pitchy contestant was pushing him toward breaking his end of the deal with Cammie.

"Okay, even I have to admit this one is a little hard to watch," she said as she got up and went into the kitchen. She returned with two beers and handed him one. "This should help."

He chuckled as he opened his and took a swig. Spending time with Cammie was like spending time with an old friend, but with an exciting dash of physical attraction sprinkled in. She wasn't overly affectionate, but Will knew that was her personality and had nothing to do with him specifically. She'd been that way with everyone she'd dated since he'd known her. He was used to more physical touch in a relationship, but for now he was just glad to be spending time with someone he genuinely enjoyed. It was a welcome change from whiling away the hours alone trying fruitlessly to forget about Evelyn and his mother. He'd been in a serious rut until a few days ago when Cammie had given him something positive to think about and work toward.

On that note, Will couldn't help but compare Cammie's and Evelyn's tastes in television. He and Evelyn had spent many hours on the couch together watching different shows and movies. His mind wandered to their first night together and how shocked he'd been when he found out her favorite movie was *Blazing Saddles*. *American Idol* was a far cry from the satirical genius that was Mel Brooks, but Will was having fun nonetheless and was glad to endure a bit of aural torture at the hands of the *Idol* contestants if it gave him the dose of happiness he'd so sorely needed all these months.

"I'm glad we're hanging out tonight," Cammie said, interrupting his thoughts. "It's good to see you smile."

"I was just thinking the same thing. A nurse *and* a mind reader! You are a woman of many talents."

"I'm serious!" She scoffed, playfully smacking his arm. "I know things have been really difficult, and I'm glad I can help, even if it's in a way we never expected."

"I appreciate that." He nodded. "Cheers."

They smiled at each other as they clinked their bottles together and took a sip.

Cammie stood up and stretched. "I'm moving to the couch. Feel free to join me."

Straight shooter.

He got up and took their dinner plates to the kitchen before sitting down next to her. He'd been much better about cleaning up the last few days. Will intentionally sat a respectable distance away from Cammie, unsure how to proceed. Once again, she solved the mystery for him.

"Come cuddle with me." She patted the couch cushion next to her.

He silently moved closer to her and put his arm around her, making himself comfortable as she nuzzled into him, serenaded by an *Idol* front-runner who Will had to admit wasn't all that bad. He wasn't used to being with a woman who was as blunt as Cammie. There was no mystery about her. She wore her heart on her sleeve and asked directly for the things she wanted. She didn't overcomplicate anything, and the only baggage she seemed to come with was the same baggage he himself carried, save for the loss of a mother. He was finding it surprisingly easy to go down a romantic path with Cammie in spite of his concerns about Evelyn. She was still in the back of his mind, but he'd made peace with the fact that she would want him to find love again, even if it was in an unexpected place.

By the end of the night, the two had finished off a couple of beers each and were both feeling a bit light on their feet. They'd started playing a game of cards, and after a few heated rounds, Cammie won the game.

"And what do I win?" she inquired.

Will pretended to be deep in thought. "Well, I don't have a trophy on hand . . ."

She laughed as she stood up. "I had something else in mind, actually."

"Oh?"

She walked toward his bedroom door, turning back to look at him when she reached it. "Yeah, a few hours of uninterrupted sleep! I worked a twelve-hour shift today. I'm too exhausted to walk home. Are you coming?"

Will felt his stomach rise into his chest. He hadn't expected to share a bed with Cammie so soon into their relationship. He grabbed his drink and stood up, hesitant to be too presumptuous but curious about where she was going with this.

She glanced back at him as she disappeared into the bedroom.

He trailed after her, still shocked at the turn the evening was suddenly taking. "Are you sure?" he asked, putting his beer down on the dresser. He'd had a few drinks and wanted to keep as clear a head as he could to navigate this situation with Cammie. "I don't want you to do anything you wouldn't do if we weren't drinking."

"We don't have to do anything at all. I just want to sleep." She sat on the edge of the bed and kicked off her shoes. "There's another singing show on, if you'd rather?"

"No!" he cried, diving under the covers. He looked up and smiled when he realized she was kidding. "How about a nice, music-free sitcom?" He picked up the remote for the bedroom TV and clicked some buttons. Cammie rested her head on his chest as they watched reruns of

Friends and chatted about everything and nothing for a while. Eventually, she started falling asleep and warned Will she might not last much longer.

He turned out the lights and lowered the volume on the television. "Do you need anything? Water?"

She stumbled over her answer, as though she was surprised at his kindness. "No thanks, I'm fine."

Will settled in and watched the show on his own as Cammie slept next to him. The date had gone better than he could have imagined but differently than he'd envisioned. His eyelids soon became heavy, and he turned off the TV before pulling the covers over himself and lying down. He closed his eyes and drifted off, content with the way things were going.

The morning sun assaulted Will's eyes earlier than he would have liked. He batted them open slowly and grinned, rolling over to greet Cammie.

"What the hell?" he whispered to himself when he saw the empty bed. He got up and walked out into the living room. Cammie wasn't there either, and the kitchen was empty. He scanned the apartment and caught sight of a piece of paper with a note scrawled on it held in place by an empty beer bottle on the coffee table. He hurried over and picked it up.

You were right. I shouldn't have spent the night. I can't do this. I'm sorry. —C

A ball of emotions bubbled up inside him, threatening to explode. He held the note in his hand and stared at it, incredulous.

"No, there's no way she's bailing on me like this. Seriously?" Will's heart was racing and somehow speaking out loud to himself seemed to put off the inevitable boiling point. "Everything was going really well! What *happened*?" Still clutching the note, he made his way to the couch and sat down, rubbing his eyes with his free hand. He let out a deep sigh and looked at it again and shook his head. He hadn't made a move on Cammie, he hadn't pushed her to do anything she didn't want to, and he thought he'd been more than understanding about the heavy circumstances of their relationship. He was suddenly regretting ever pursuing anything with her. Finally, he yelled, "What did I do wrong?! Why does everyone always leave me?!" He crumpled up the note, stood up, and squeezed it as hard as he could in his fist. He flung it across the room, letting out an angry, primal growl, and sat back down. His head in his hands, he breathed heavily until he cried as he grappled with his latest loss.

Chapter 13

1922

Evelyn and Holstead were back in his office. He had opened the new package of files from Fletch's house and was beginning to leaf through them. Evelyn watched, her mind still on Mariah. There was definitely more to the woman's tears than she had let on.

"Earlier, when I went to help Mrs. Fletcher with the tea," Evelyn said, interrupting Holstead's review of the papers, "I found her crying alone."

"Oh?" Holstead looked up, interested. "What was she upset about?"

"She said seeing you had churned up memories of Dr. Fletcher, but I get the feeling she wasn't telling me everything."

Holstead sat back in his chair. "Theirs was a complicated marriage." He folded his hands over his front as he reflected. "They always had some tension between them. Fletch didn't talk about it much to anyone, but I gathered it had a lot to do with his work. He was a bit of a one-track mind, and poor Mariah was left home alone much of the time."

Evelyn could relate to Mrs. Fletcher on that particular complaint. She and Thomas had been quarreling over the very same thing lately, and she knew how difficult it was to compete with your partner's work for their attention.

Seemingly unaware, Holstead had returned to the files, skimming briefly through them to get an idea of what was inside the well-hidden secret research papers. Evelyn watched and silently vowed to go back and visit Mariah Fletcher sometime, if for no other reason than to give the poor woman some company. But also because Evelyn felt a kinship with her. Perhaps their absent, work-obsessed partners were the reason.

Evelyn snapped back to reality when Holstead stood up suddenly, pulling some papers out of the stack. "Well, I never."

Evelyn sat up straight, eager to hear what he had found. He stayed annoyingly silent, reading to himself, until she couldn't hold in her curiosity any longer.

"What is it?" She stood up and leaned over the desk to get a better look.

Holstead held up the paperwork, which was all text. "It appears Fletch found a way for dreamers to flash forward without human contact."

"How?" Evelyn's heart was racing.

"It says here all a dreamer needs in order to experience the flashes is to touch something—a physical item—that strongly connects them to a person in their other life."

"I don't understand. Like what?"

"For example, Louis, the dreamer mentioned in Fletch's studies, owned a pocket watch that had been passed down through the generations. When he died in his later timeline, he and Fletch discovered the pocket watch was the catalyst for his flashes forward, the same way you're describing your recent visits to 2006."

Evelyn was speechless. Her mind swirled with thoughts of what items she could possibly get her hands on that would connect her to Will. The dreamer in Fletch's studies had flashed backward, making it much easier to have brought some artifact passed down through the generations over time. Evelyn had lost a life eighty-four years in the future, and artifacts didn't get handed backward in time.

She whispered to herself as she realized the answer. "I need something from Will's family."

"I'm sorry, dear? I didn't catch that," Holstead inquired, cupping his hand behind his ear.

"No, it's nothing."

Holstead carried on speaking. "Fletch's research suggests that you can flash forward anytime you desire if you find such an object. It says here some objects work better than others, but no information on how to tell which ones, or why." He paused, eyeing her carefully. "However, I should warn you that he passed away before he finished studying this. We don't know the effects of flashing between timelines too many times."

"I understand," she said, her voice barely a whisper.

"Please, Evelyn, don't do anything you'll regret." Holstead placed his hand tenderly on her arm. "I would hate to see you get hurt or for you and Thomas to fall apart over these visits to the other timeline."

"I know." She gazed down at the pile of research papers that threatened to change everything. "But I think I have to do this."

Chapter 14
2006

Will stumbled through the main doors of the emergency room at Lenox Hill Hospital at about ten thirty in the middle of a busy night shift. He had never been so drunk, but he didn't care. He didn't care about anything right now. After Cammie had left him with a break-up note that morning, Will had called out of work, pretending to be sick with a stomach bug. He looked up the hours of operation for Chasers and made a dash for the bar, arriving only a couple of minutes after Britt, another bartender Will knew there, had flipped the sign to "open." He caught her concerned glare as he walked in. "I know, it's too early. But you're open, right?"

"Hey, not my business. I'm not judging." She held up her hands in surrender and made her way behind the bar. "The usual?"

Will shook his head. "You got a bottle?"

"Of what? Champagne?" Britt cocked her head.

"Yeah."

"Of course. We never even used to stock the stuff until you started coming in. Now we always have a couple of bottles around."

"I'll take a bottle. And a glass." He hadn't stopped staring down at his hands, which were fiddling with his keys atop the bar. "Please."

Britt blinked at him a couple of times, clearly unsure whether she should comply with his request. "Are you sure? You don't usually drink that much."

He let go of the keys and they clattered onto the bartop as he looked her in the eye. "I'm sure."

Now, approaching the front desk at the Lenox Hill ER, Will was on a mission. The older woman doing check-in, whose name tag read Lena, looked up at him, smiling at first. "What can I do for you?" When she saw the disheveled young man, she became straight-faced.

Will leaned clumsily against the desk. "I'm looking for Cammie."

"Cammie? Cammie who?"

"The nurse! Cammie! She works here." Will ran his hands through his hair, agitated. "I know she's here. Just lemme in so I can talk to her!"

"Sir, that's not how it works. I can—"

Will slammed his hands on Lena's desk and shouted at the top of his lungs, "Cammie! C-A-M-M-I-E! I need to talk to her!"

As Lena reached for the phone to call security, the locked doors separating the waiting room from the triage area opened, and Cammie appeared, her eyes wide and her mouth agape when she saw Will in his drunken state.

She walked quickly toward him, her face bright red with embarrassment. She grabbed his upper arm and pulled him through the double doors she'd come from.

"What the hell are you doing?" she snapped. "Are you trying to get me fired?"

"I want you to take this stupid note back!" He produced the crumpled break-up note from his pocket.

"Will, this isn't the right time to talk about this." She begged him with her eyes as well as her words. "Please, I'm working. Can we do this later?"

He scoffed. "Sure, we'll talk later." He waved his arms dramatically, mocking her. As he did, he lost his balance and stumbled backward, tripping over an IV pole. His back of his head hit the metal handrail along the wall before he fell to the ground with a loud thud.

Cammie cried out and bent down to check on him. His eyes were closed and he was unresponsive. She called out for help.

Soon, Will was in a hospital bed, an IV pumping fluids into him to sober him up and rehydrate him, a doctor checking for signs of concussion. Cammie had to move on to her other patients. She stared at him from the entrance of his room before she left.

As he pretended to sleep, Will heard Cammie whisper to herself, "This would never have happened if Evelyn were still here."

Chapter 15

1922

Back at her apartment, Evelyn searched frantically to find an object that could connect her back to Will. She wasn't even sure what she was expecting to find if she flashed forward again. She just couldn't shake the need to learn more about his relationship with Cammie. Her brain had been running through all the possibilities since she'd seen them together at the coffee shop. Maybe she'd seen it wrong and they were just friends? Maybe they were married and living happily ever after. As much as the latter made Evelyn's heart drop, she had to visit 2006 again to figure it out. She hated to admit it, but in the back of her mind was the idea that if Cammie and Will were indeed in love and headed for a life together, it might provide the closure she needed to move forward with Thomas without any "what ifs" or regrets.

Naturally, objects were not passed down backward through time, so she had a hard time coming up with anything—besides Cecil—that might have a strong enough physical connection to her other timeline—and to Will—to flash her forward again. After rifling through her jewelry and drawers, she had an idea.

Evelyn flung the closet door open once again and tossed aside the stack of shoe boxes that had previously hidden her most recent journal. She hadn't bothered hiding it again since Thomas had found it. She didn't see much point since he already knew what was going on. What he didn't know was that at the bottom of that pile was a shoe box that contained another of her journals. The one she'd kept during the time she'd gone back and forth between Thomas in 1919 and Will in 2003. When she'd had to let Will go and carry on here.

She hadn't looked at the journal since she'd died in the other life. She couldn't bear to read through all her memories of Will and their perfect, whirlwind relationship. It was too hard to think about what could have been if they hadn't been interrupted by the loss of her dreams. Planting herself on the floor in front of the closet, she carefully unwrapped the journal, her adrenaline picking up.

As she revealed the cover, her eyes instantly started swimming in tears. The mere sight of the book's soft, green leather brought her back to a time when she'd had more love in both her lives than she knew what to do with. When she had the effortless, passionate, reliable love of Will Jenkins. She hadn't been the same since she'd lost it.

She forced herself to return to the task at hand and opened the journal. As she leafed through the pages slowly, she tried not to read much, but the memories came flooding back nonetheless. She finally found the page she was looking for. She didn't even have to read it to know it was the right one. She could recite it by heart. It was the entry she'd written the day Will had first told her he loved her.

Opening the journal wide, she placed it on the floor next to her and closed her eyes as she pressed her hand firmly against her writing from three years ago.

The white light consumed her momentarily before it dissipated, but it wasn't as dazzling as it had been the first two times. When it was gone, Evelyn was in a hospital. She couldn't imagine why she would be sent here looking for Will, but her presence in this timeline with the journal as her conduit felt almost like a radio that couldn't quite settle on a frequency. Her connection to 2006 wasn't as strong as it had been when she'd touched Cecil, and she knew she didn't have much time to figure out where Will was or what was going on between him and Cammie. Trying to stay here was physically draining, and her body was fully aware of the effects. Everything hurt. Evelyn gasped when it hit her that Cammie might be in this hospital, working.

Just then, a nurse pulled back a curtain to one of the ER rooms, revealing to Evelyn the one thing she'd hoped *not* to find here: Will, lying in a hospital bed.

Panic instantly coursed through her body, and at the same time, she couldn't quite get her brain to fully focus on this timeline. She was desperate to stay longer and find out what had happened to Will, but as much as she didn't want to leave, she had to end this visit and find a better way.

Evelyn's breath sputtered as she took her hand off the journal and came back fully to her bedroom in 1922. Her heart drummed in her chest. What was wrong with Will, and why was he in the emergency room? Every bit of her wanted to go back to him and make sure he was going to be fine, but the journal obviously wasn't enough to get her all the way there to stay awhile. She needed something else and wished more than anything she could go to Cecil and hold his hand for as long as she needed to. A simple handshake had been enough to get her to Will the last two times. As a realization hit her, she sat up straight and tossed the journal onto the bed. She hadn't actually touched Cecil's hand the second time she'd seen him. She'd touched his arm. His *coat*.

She stood up and hastily pulled on her gloves, grabbed her bag, and rushed out of the apartment.

Evelyn arrived outside the bank just fifteen minutes before it was due to close for the day. She hoped Cecil hadn't left yet. Taking the stairs up to the grand entrance to the bank lobby, she wrapped her scarf around her neck and covered her face the best she could without looking suspicious. She entered the bank and took a quick look around. To her right was a counter where customers were scribbling deposit and withdrawal forms, hurrying to get their banking done before the end of the day. To her left was the open entrance to a large coat closet. Evelyn ducked inside and quickly began sifting through the coats hanging on the rack. She noticed after a few seconds that some of the hangers had names on them for the bank's employees. She said a silent thank you to the universe for making her job a little easier as she searched eagerly for Cecil's name. She finally found his coat, almost the last one on the rack. She checked to make sure no one was coming and hurriedly grabbed it, balling it up so no one would recognize it, and slunk out of the closet. Careful not to attract any attention, she calmly strolled through the lobby doors, then hurried down the stairs. The coat in her hands, she dashed home to test her theory.

Chapter 16
2006

Will had just woken up when Cammie came into his room to check on him in the emergency department.

"I'm surprised to see you awake so soon. How are you feeling?" she asked, making her way to his bedside to adjust his IV.

Will sat up and pushed the hair out of his eyes, still groggy. "Fine, I think? Is it too embarrassing to admit I don't exactly remember what happened?"

"You came in here looking for me and fell. You hit your head pretty hard, but the doctor says you're lucky. No concussion."

"I'm so stupid." He covered his face with his hands. "I don't know what came over me. I've never had that much to drink in my life. I am *so* sorry, Cammie." He removed his hands from his face and closed his eyes. "This isn't me."

"You always were a lightweight." Will rolled his eyes and smiled and Cammie stifled a laugh, then got back to the point. "No, seriously, I should apologize, as well. I never should have left you with a stupid note. I should have waited and talked to you face to face. *I'm* sorry."

He opened his eyes again. "I guess the note was the tipping point for me, but it still doesn't excuse the way I acted. I never drink like that. Maybe two or three, usually, but not like that. I ordered a whole bottle of champagne. I really am sorry for embarrassing you at work. I hope I didn't get you into any trouble."

She finished fiddling with the machines and looked at him. "I forgive you," she said, "but this isn't gonna work, is it?"

"You mean us?"

"It's obviously causing you way too much stress. I don't think it's good for you."

He sighed in defeat. "I know you're right. I just hate that I can't seem to move on in a healthy way."

Cammie sat down on the edge of the bed and folded her hands in her lap. "You've been through so much, Will. It's okay to not be okay right now."

"Yeah. That's what everyone says." He closed his eyes and let out a long, hopeless breath.

"You know, we don't have to be together romantically for me to help you through it all. I was your friend first. I still am."

He looked directly at her for the first time since she'd come in. He wished their being together wasn't so wrought with emotional complications, but here they were. In an impossible, difficult situation with only one clear answer that wouldn't hurt anyone too much in the end. They had to be just friends. He'd accept it even if he didn't like it, and she would, too.

"I mean it," she said. "As your friend, I'm always only a phone call away, I promise. If you ever feel like you're on the brink of breaking down, call me. We can still hang out without it being weird between us. Right?"

"I'd like that," he said hoarsely.

She smiled at him and lowered herself off the bed. "I have to get to work. I'll be back in a bit. You'll probably be discharged soon." She headed toward the door.

"Cammie?" She turned and looked back at him. "Thank you." He smiled faintly. "And I'm sorry again for being so loud and making a scene."

She scoffed and waved him away. "It's a city hospital. Trust me, we've seen so much worse!"

Chapter 17

1922

Evelyn was finally home after her trip to the bank to steal Cecil's coat. She'd never stolen anything in her life, and the guilt would be eating her alive if it weren't for the high stakes attached. She hung the coat carefully on the rack by the front door and made sure not to touch it without gloves until she was ready to flash forward. She set an alarm to go off in exactly one hour, hoping it would act as a failsafe in case she was unable to find her way back and get the coat off. Holstead's warnings about the physical impact on her body from traveling to 2006 were still on her mind. She wasn't even sure yet if the coat would work to flash her forward to Will, but she wanted to be prepared in case it did.

Her body and mind were still feeling a bit weak and wobbly after her last attempt to flash forward with the journal, so she took a moment to drink a glass of water before she tried again. After chugging it, her hands still gloved, Evelyn brought the coat into her bedroom and sat on the bed. She slowly took off the gloves and placed them beside her. Taking a deep breath, she picked up the coat and draped it around her shoulders.

She soon found herself on the other side of the white light and firmly in the bedroom of a modern New York City apartment she didn't recognize. The coat's connection to this timeline was significantly stronger than her journal had been. There was no one else around that she could see. Evelyn searched for clues that would tell her whether or not this was where Will lived. The walls were undecorated, and stacks of boxes occupied the corners of the apartment, which was furnished minimally. When they were together in 2003, he'd lined his walls with music and movie posters and displayed photos of his parents. He'd even framed a photo of himself with Evelyn and hung it up before she'd passed. If this was his place now, she hoped he'd just moved in.

She went into the living room to find some evidence that she was in the right place. Almost instantly her eye was drawn to a strange-looking vase on the mantle above an electric fireplace. When she got closer and read the inscription on the plaque at the bottom, her jaw dropped.

"*Lynn Jenkins. 1958-2005.*" It was an urn.

Evelyn stuffed down a sudden sob that lurched into her throat at the idea of Will shouldering so much loss in such a short time. His mother had died within just two years of Evelyn's own death date. She couldn't imagine how much he must have suffered emotionally and became even more worried about what might have landed him in the hospital. She stared at the urn, wondering how she could get to Will. If he was still in the hospital, she needed to know what was wrong with him.

"Who are you?"

Evelyn whipped around as fast as her body would allow. His voice sounded like music, and she would know it anywhere.

"Will!" She could hardly get the word out, but a whisper found its way from her mouth.

He had a white bath towel wrapped around his waist, his skin glistening from the shower. His mouth was agape, and his gorgeous eyes darted up and down as he took in what he thought he was seeing. His face had gone pale. She was dressed in 1920s clothing and her hair was cut shorter, but surely he'd still recognize her.

"Evelyn?" He inched toward her. "Is this real?"

She wanted to reassure him she was really there, but she was frozen to the spot and afraid to speak in case she scared him. The fact that he could see her, that he was speaking to her, was the most painfully exquisite thing she'd ever experienced. She had no idea if it would last, but she was eternally thankful for this moment where they could see and feel each other once more. She'd felt robbed of looking into his eyes for the rest of her life when she'd died three years ago, and staring into them now, they were just as magical as she remembered. He finally stood directly in front of her, close enough that she could see the gold flecks in them. Her breath was shaky as he reached out his hand and hesitantly touched his fingertips to her cheek, confirming she was truly there. She gasped when she felt his warm flesh against hers, and a lone tear fell from one of his eyes and made its way down his face.

"It's really you?"

She hadn't even noticed her own tears beginning to fall. "It's me, Will! It's really me!"

They both sobbed as they launched into an embrace so tight their muscles hurt from holding each other. He pulled back and looked at her, her face in his hands, and wiped the tears from her cheeks. She was trembling with happiness as she took in his hair, his lips, his skin. She had missed him so much more than she'd even realized.

"How is this possible?" he asked. "How are you here? This isn't real. I have to be dreaming." He began breathing fast, panicking. "I'm hallucinating." He sat on the edge of the bed, rubbing his hands over his face, trying to catch his breath.

Evelyn crouched in front of him and took his hands. "Will! It's really happening! I swear!" She gripped his upper arms and tried to look him in the eye, desperate for him to believe. "I found a way to travel here and see you from the other timeline!"

He ran his hand through his hair and took a deep breath in, trying to focus. "How?"

"It's a long story." She got up and sat on the bed next to him and tried to steady her own breathing. "I can't believe it actually worked. God, I've missed you so, so much!" She hugged him again and didn't let go for several moments. They sat, wrapped in each other's arms, relishing the moment as if it were both their first and their last. Because they already knew what that really meant, and they'd never take a second together for granted ever again, no matter how many or few they had.

Finally, they pulled away. "Are you back?" The hope in his voice cut Evelyn's heart like a knife.

"I'm afraid not."

His shoulders fell in disappointment.

"But I think I figured out a way for me to visit anytime I want."

"I don't understand."

Evelyn explained the flashes and Fletcher's secret research as briefly as she could. Will was incredulous, especially when she told him she'd met Cecil.

"Cecil Jenkins is my great-grandfather!" He blinked in disbelief. "He passed that coat down to my dad, and my mom kept it for me. I just got it a few months ago. It's in my storage unit. I used to wear it every time we visited him when I was little. I'd pretend I was a detective. This is wild!"

"Cecil looks exactly like you. He's a really nice man. It obviously runs in the family." She smiled coyly at him, knowing he must have missed her brand of humor.

"Sitting here with you, it feels like no time has passed. Am I dreaming?" He paused and stared at her longingly. "I don't know if I can let you go again."

"I do have to go soon." Her face fell as she remembered she'd set her alarm. "I don't know yet how long the flashes last, or what happens if I stay too long. Holstead and I are working on it."

He took her hand in his and kissed it. "I don't want you to go, but I'll take every second I can get."

Evelyn suddenly recalled seeing the urn. "I'm so sorry about your mom," she said quietly. "I wish I could have been here for you."

His demeanor changed the instant she mentioned his mother's death. He very obviously hadn't worked through his grief yet.

He studied the floor. "She was way too young. Just like you."

"She was so lucky to have had you. We both were." Evelyn squeezed his hand.

He sniffed and exhaled sharply. "And now I'm alone."

Evelyn stopped herself from blurting out something about Cammie. She couldn't seem to find the right words, anyway.

"Okay, no more pity party!" Will said, standing up. "I have something you might remember." He walked over to his dresser and opened the top drawer, retrieving something from the front corner. He came back to Evelyn, his hand outstretched to give her what he was holding. She opened her palm to receive it, and when she looked down to see what it was, she almost cried again. It was the champagne cork from their most romantic date night at a beautiful mansion in the city. She'd given it to him to keep the moment before she died. She swallowed. "How could I forget?"

"Now that you can come back, it doesn't have to be one of our last memories anymore." He sat back down next to her. "We're going to make so many more."

A wave of jealousy and sadness overcame her as she once again recalled seeing him with Cammie at the coffee shop a few days before. She had to know. "Will, I have to ask you something."

"Anything."

She hesitated, unsure how to bring it up. "Are you and Cammie . . . I mean, is she your—"

"Whoa. Cammie and I are *not* together. Not like that. We tried it out for like, a minute, because we were both feeling vulnerable. It didn't work out. That was the end. I swear."

Evelyn wanted to be angry, but he hadn't actually done anything wrong, no matter how much it tore her apart inside. "I believe you."

"Cammie has been a really good friend to me. That's it. The whole thing was my fault. I was drinking, and I took it too far. She was just trying to help me." He paused. "How did you even know about that?"

"I've managed to make a couple of very brief visits before this one."

"Oh. I'm really sorry you had to see that. It really is over."

Evelyn hated hearing about it, but her muscles relaxed upon learning their fling was brief. And over. Besides, she hadn't stayed loyal to Will in her timeline, either. They didn't owe each other that. For all they had both known, they were never going to see each other again. Still, she had to tell him she was engaged to Thomas in her other world. She toyed with her ring, which Will hadn't noticed yet, as she contemplated how to deliver the news. She hated the thought of hurting him again, but if she was going to come back and see him—and she hoped she could, even just as friends—he had to know where things stood.

"Will, you should know—"

Before Evelyn could finish her sentence, she found herself whisked out of Will's apartment in a flash of bright light and back into her own home in 1922. Her alarm clock was blaring on the nightstand next to her. Evelyn propped herself up on her elbow from where she'd been lying and turned it off. Cecil's coat had slid off the bed and crumpled into a heap on the floor. She was heartbroken to be away from Will again. Especially without a proper goodbye.

Evelyn took stock of herself to evaluate the toll the visit had taken on her body, heeding Holstead's warning that the flashes may be physically taxing. Her head was pounding a bit, and she was weak. Her legs were shaking, but otherwise she felt relatively normal. As much as she wanted to go back to Will immediately, she knew she should err on the side of caution and wait to find out more from Holstead before she flashed forward on her own again too soon.

She put on her gloves and carefully picked up the coat to hang it in her closet. As she did, she noticed something fall out of it and onto the floor. She bent down to pick up the stray object, which had rolled under the bed. Evelyn knelt down and felt around in the darkness until her hand settled on whatever had dropped from Cecil's jacket. When she pulled it out from under the bed and opened her palm to see what it was, she cried out in shock.

It was the cork from Will's apartment.

Chapter 18

1922

Evelyn couldn't knock on Mariah Fletcher's door fast enough. She'd come as early as she reasonably could. She was dying to get back into the Fletchers' house and that office.

Finding the cork in her bedroom had shaken Evelyn to her core. Not only had she been able to visit 2006, she'd been able to bring back a physical item from that timeline to 1922 with her. She'd been up all night imagining what it all meant. She couldn't help but wonder: if she could bring back a cork, could she bring back a person?

The door opened and Mariah's kind face peered out. "Evelyn! How lovely to see you again!"

Evelyn smiled back as Mrs. Fletcher ushered her inside. "I hope it's not too early to call on you," she said, removing her coat.

"Not at all! I'm glad to have the company. Follow me to the kitchen. I was just about to make some tea."

"I was in the area and couldn't pass by without stopping to say hello." Evelyn was fibbing, but she had no choice. And she genuinely did like Mariah. On any other day, she really might have stopped in for a friendly visit. Today, she was here on business.

Mariah gestured for Evelyn to enter the kitchen ahead of her. "I admit I have been looking forward to visiting with you again. I so enjoyed our chat the other day. It was nice to have someone to talk to."

"I enjoyed it as well."

"I hope the files you and Walter found proved helpful." Mariah filled the kettle.

"Oh, yes, thank you. More than you know." Evelyn arranged the cups and saucers on a tea tray. "The research we have is full of useful information, of course, but seems . . . incomplete?" Evelyn paused and glanced at Mariah to gauge her reaction before she continued. Mariah didn't appear fazed so far. "I was actually hoping you might be able to tell me where I could find even more files your husband may have kept. Doctor Holstead would have come, but he's feeling a bit under the weather, so he sent me instead." The lies were adding up fast. Holstead was fine, and Evelyn hated bringing his name into her ruse, but she was determined to find answers about her abilities now that she'd found out she could indeed transport physical objects from one timeline to the other. Besides, in the grand scheme of things, this lie was far less grave than some of the others she'd been telling lately.

"I'm not sure what I can do to help." Mariah was searching for something in a kitchen cabinet. "My husband never shared with me where he kept any of his research."

Evelyn's face fell. She knew there had to be something more to what Fletcher had learned about the flashes before he passed away. Her gut was telling her whatever secret Fletch had hidden was the key to finding out if there was a way for her to be with Will again. It was a long shot, and she knew she was playing with fire, but her love for Will hadn't changed a bit, and spending time with him the night before had only solidified for her that he was her soulmate and it was worth everything to explore all her options. Especially before she married Thomas.

"Shall we go to the sitting room?" Mariah suggested, picking up the tea tray and heading for the kitchen door.

Once they were settled and had poured their tea, Evelyn made one last, hopeful campaign to search the office. She took a sip and swallowed before she blurted out the thing she knew could change the way Mariah looked at her forever.

"Mrs. Fletcher, I'm a dreamer."

Their eyes met in a silent stare that almost frightened Evelyn. She wasn't sure what reaction was coming on the other side of the look Mariah was giving her, but her heart was racing in anticipation.

After what seemed like eons, Mariah smiled. "I'd guessed that."

Evelyn's forehead wrinkled. "You knew?"

"I've met enough of them to know." Mariah shrugged. "And Walter bringing you here was a rather strong hint."

"I suppose we weren't as discreet as we thought." Evelyn sighed. "I'm sorry. I wasn't trying to lie to you or bring any turmoil into your life. I just never know how anyone will react when they find out."

Mariah chuckled. "You don't have to worry about me. The dreamers have been a big part of my life." She paused and looked down at her teacup. "My marriage, even."

Evelyn raised her eyebrows. Her interest was piqued.

"I really shouldn't speak ill of the dead, should I?" Mariah forced a quiet laugh as she stirred her tea for the third time since they'd sat down. Evelyn could tell there was so much Mrs. Fletcher wasn't saying to her, but she didn't want to pry. She also still wanted to look through Fletch's office one more time.

"My fiancé is a doctor, as well," Evelyn said, hoping to bridge any gap that was still between them. A touch of sadness washed over her when she remembered Thomas wasn't technically her fiancé at the moment, but it was all too much to explain to Mariah, and not the right time. "I'm quickly learning how difficult it is to share your partner with the real love of his life: his work."

"I certainly know a thing or two about that!"

The women shared a laugh before Evelyn went in for the kill.

"I think whatever additional research Doctor Fletcher might have stashed away in his office could determine if my future is with my fiancé or not. I really need to get back into that office and see if I can find something that would help me. Please."

Mrs. Fletcher put down her tea and looked directly at Evelyn. "My dear, a word of advice, if I may?" Evelyn nodded and put her own cup down. "Sometimes the answers we're looking for are more upsetting than they are comforting. Are you *sure* you want to know more and risk everything you've built?"

Evelyn opened her mouth to answer but couldn't seem to form the right words. She was willing to do whatever it took to find the answers, but she didn't want to hurt anyone in the process. Especially poor Thomas.

Mariah filled the silence. "Fletcher risked it all to find answers about the dreamers once. And it broke us."

"How?"

Now it was Mariah's turn to struggle to find the right words. Eventually, she stood up. "I know where to find the answers you're looking for. But I need to know, Evelyn: are you absolutely *certain* you're ready?"

Chapter 19

2006

Will hadn't been able to stop thinking about Evelyn's visit. Sleep had evaded him the entire night after she'd appeared in his apartment. He was struggling to convince himself he hadn't lost his mind and that it had actually happened. What he'd experienced should be impossible, and yet he'd touched her. Talked to her again. Breathed her in. Less than an hour with her and his entire world had turned upside down. He needed to know when she'd be back. *If* she'd be back. Waiting to find out what was next was killing him. He was anxious to take action instead of just idly waiting for Evelyn's next visit. Finally, he had an idea. It was a long shot, but it was worth a try.

Thankfully it was Saturday, so he didn't have to call out of work this time. He spent an hour on his computer and making phone calls and soon found an address for a Mrs. Caroline Huber in Saugerties upstate. Caroline was a dreamer he and Evelyn had tracked down a few years ago when they were looking for a way to prevent Evelyn from losing her life in this timeline. They'd gone to Caroline's church and talked to her, but their discussion had been interrupted. He wanted to talk to Caroline again. She had lost her dreams, like Evelyn, and Will was hopeful she had experienced the flashes and could tell him how they worked.

Will called and booked a rental car. He'd sold his own car after his mother had passed away. The only reason he'd kept it when he'd come to school in the city was so he could drive back to Ohio and see her. Within an hour, Will had picked up the rental and was on the road to Saugerties. He hoped Caroline was of sound enough mind to help him. Last time he'd seen her he hadn't been so sure.

It was a long, boring drive, and Will had considered inviting Cammie along to keep him company, but he figured she could use a break from him. If he was being honest with himself, the drive reminded him of Evelyn. They'd made this trip together on another rainy day three years ago. He'd promised her on that drive that he was going to save her. He was still angry with himself for not being able to keep that promise. This was his chance to fix it.

After exiting the highway, he finally turned onto Caroline's street and slowed down, squinting to read the house numbers through the raindrops on the car windows. He parked and pulled the hood of his jacket up as he jogged up the path to Caroline's front door. Biting his lip nervously, he rang the doorbell, taking refuge from the rain under the cover of the front porch. When the door cracked open, the face of a middle-aged woman stared back at him. "May I help you?"

Will was taken aback. He'd shot up to Caroline's house so fast he hadn't even taken the time to think of what he would say if someone else answered the door. He knew he couldn't lead with telling her he wanted to talk to Caroline about time traveling back to 1922. As he stuttered and stumbled to come up with something on the fly, the door opened wider, and Caroline peeked over the younger woman's shoulder.

"I remember you!" she cried. "I saw you at the church!"

Soon Will was sitting in Caroline Huber's living room waiting for the other woman, who it turned out was Caroline's daughter, Lydia, to make them some coffee. Will wasn't sure where to begin.

"I know it's odd, me showing up here like this," he said, nervously fidgeting with the edge of the upholstered armchair in which he was seated.

"No." Caroline smiled. "I knew you and Evelyn had more questions for me that day at the church."

"We were afraid we'd upset you." Will recalled how Caroline's caregiver had whisked her away from them in the church yard.

"I had just had a fall in my shower and hit my head a few weeks before I saw you back then," Caroline explained. "Everyone was so worried about me all the time. They got me a nurse. She was sweet, but I didn't need that much attention, really. Always watching and listening. Constantly making me sit and lie down. Thank goodness I finally convinced everyone I was perfectly capable on my own, and now they've let up a bit. My daughter still makes sure I'm well taken care of, of course." Caroline beamed toward Lydia, who had entered the room with two steaming cups of coffee. She handed one to Will, eyeing him intently. It was obvious Lydia was unsure about his visit. He wanted to reassure her and tell her he just had questions about the dreamer research, but he didn't know if Caroline's daughter even knew she was a dreamer. He'd learned from Evelyn that many of the dreamers didn't broadcast their abilities for various reasons, not the least of which being that to anyone who didn't know better, their traveling back and forth between two timelines sounded like the stuff of fairy tales or the ramblings of a madman. To his relief, Lydia excused herself to go and fold some laundry, leaving Will and Caroline to talk privately.

"I almost don't want to ask, because I'm afraid I already know the answer," Caroline said, stirring her coffee. "But where is Evelyn?" Will's expression must have told Caroline all she needed to know. "I'm sorry. When did it happen?"

"A few weeks after we saw you at the church."

"And since you're here now, I have to assume you're looking for information about the daydreams."

Will sat up straighter. "Daydreams?"

"That's what I call them. I'm not sure if they have a real name, but I call them daydreams. You go to your old life by touching something or someone with a strong connection to your past. I actually had a very brief daydream myself when I touched Evelyn's arm at the church." She glanced at Will, who was staring straight ahead, processing everything she'd just said. She continued. "You've seen Evelyn, I take it?"

"Yes," Will said softly. He was having a hard time containing the sudden torrent of emotions that washed over him when he acknowledged out loud for the first time that he'd seen and talked to the love of his life, who had been dead for the better part of three years. Talking to someone openly about the dreamers was freeing after having to mask it for so long. He'd spent all the time since Evelyn's death pretending to blame it on some bogus medical issue. "She called them flashes." He paused, wrinkling his forehead as he put something together. "Is that what you meant at the church when you told Evelyn the dreams weren't really going to end?"

"Yes. I didn't know how to explain it to her with that nurse fawning over me, but I wanted to warn her. How long did she manage to stay when she visited you?"

"Less than an hour." He swallowed hard to keep from crying. "She said she'd be back, but I'm terrified she'll never be able to visit again and I'll just be waiting. For the rest of my life, always waiting and hoping for her to pop up at any moment."

"She'll come back," Caroline said matter-of-factly. "It's easy to come back."

"But she can't stay?"

"I'm afraid the daydreams do take a toll. On both your body and your mind. The longer she stays here, the more depleted her body will be on the other side when she returns."

He sighed with disappointment. "I don't want her to get hurt."

"She will do what she wants to do. And Evelyn is strong. She of all the dreamers will manage to visit as often as she can."

Will froze, his coffee cup halfway to his lips. "What does that mean?"

Caroline chuckled softly. "The Evelyn I knew in the 1900s was the most powerful dreamer I ever saw."

Chapter 20

1922

Evelyn walked home carrying a decorative cardboard box Mariah Fletcher had given to her. She had no idea what was inside it, but the way Mariah had tried to prepare her for its contents had her thoughts shooting off in all directions. Mariah insisted Evelyn open the box in private. Evelyn couldn't wait to get home and find out what secret about the dreamers Doctor Fletcher had hidden away so carefully that even his most trusted partner and friend, Doctor Holstead, hadn't been privy to it.

She hurried into her building, made anxious small talk with Edward on the way up to her floor, and finally burst through her apartment door. Haphazardly throwing her coat on the couch, she sat down and placed the box on the coffee table. As she untied the twine that had been tightly wrapped around it to keep it sealed, Evelyn's hands shook slightly. She knew without a doubt she was about to uncover information that might change everything. She placed her hands on either side of the box and held her breath as she prepared to lift the lid.

A sudden knock on the door made her jump. She grabbed the box and jammed it into a low kitchen cabinet on her way to answer the door. Whoever was outside certainly didn't need to be part of learning what was inside it.

Evelyn paused before unlocking and opening the door. She'd been mugged a few years prior, and ever since, she didn't take many chances with safety if she could help it. "Who's there?" she called through the door.

"It's me!"

Her stomach jumped. *Thomas.* The fact that he hadn't used his key and had knocked on the door was a stinging reminder that their engagement was off.

After an awkward greeting at the door, he came in and they stood in the living room facing each other, struggling for where to begin. They hadn't talked in a few days, and their last interaction had been tense, to say the least. Evelyn was surprised at how nervous she felt around him after their latest fight, considering she had been engaged to him just days before. The stakes were high, and they were both acutely aware of it.

"I'm sorry I've been out of touch," Thomas began. "I . . . I assumed you would want some space, so I've been throwing myself into work." He wiped a little sweat off his forehead. Evelyn was surprised he was also so highly strung.

"It's all right." Evelyn fidgeted with her engagement ring, unsure of what else to say. If she was honest, she'd been so distracted with the flashes to 2006 that she hadn't given her fight with Thomas as much thought as she probably should have. "I should have reached out, as well."

"I've been thinking a lot. About your . . . visits."

"The flashes."

"Yes, the flashes." He sighed. "I think I've been unfair. And too hard on you."

She made direct eye contact with him for the first time since he'd arrived. "That's the last thing I expected you to say."

He continued. "You didn't ask to be a dreamer. It's not your fault you have these abilities."

"You didn't ask for it, either."

"I asked you to marry me knowing you were a dreamer. I knew I had to accept everything that came along with it."

"Even if it's tearing you apart?"

"Even if it's tearing me apart."

Evelyn was tongue-tied trying to come up with a response. The scenario was eerily familiar. She'd fought with Thomas over her connection with Will back in 1919 before she'd lost her other life. Thomas had been so jealous of Will he'd left her sitting in a donut shop crying. The tension in the air between them now was as palpable as it had been then, perhaps even more so. The idea that she could once again be thrust into a situation where she'd have to choose between the two men she loved was more than she could bear.

"What do we do now?" she asked.

"I was hoping I would apologize for acting so crazy, and then you'd forgive me."

"And then?"

He came closer and took her hands in his. "And then . . . we'd start planning our wedding. Really planning it. I mean it."

Evelyn knew she should be overjoyed. She'd been begging him to get serious about their wedding for months, and it had been a major source of conflict between them. They'd set a vague date—sometime in spring—and decided they would be married in Virginia, where Evelyn's parents lived. Evelyn had looked at a few magazines to get ideas for a dress, but Thomas's work and the expense of the new office had kept them from doing anything more when it came to the wedding. A week ago, she would have jumped for joy at hearing him say he was ready to dive into planning. Now, she wasn't so sure. Something about his sudden change of heart was gnawing at the back of her mind. His palms were clammy as he held her hands. If he was being completely honest, why was he still so anxious? She told herself he was likely concerned about his ability to live up to his own promises, given his tight schedule. "What about your work?"

"I'll make the time, I swear."

"We have other problems, you know. The apartment, money, my job. The flashes."

"I know. The apartment and the job will come right in time."

"What about the flashes, Thomas?"

He let go of her hands and walked to the sofa. He sat with his arms crossed. "I suppose I'll have to just learn to turn a blind eye to the fact that my wife has another love, in another life, that she could choose to visit any time she likes."

Her heart sank. "You said you could never do that. And it's not what I want for you."

He sat up straight and looked at her, his jaw set and his eyes stern. "I love you, Evelyn. And I've always known what loving you means. I can learn to live with it."

Evelyn was still battling with herself to make sense of the stark difference between what Thomas was telling her today and what he'd said last time they'd talked. She hoped he wasn't settling for her in spite of his misgivings about the flashes and Will. Maybe he was afraid he wouldn't be able to find someone else. His mother had always said he never really pursued women or even had many friends before Evelyn had come along. A painful lump was forming in her throat threatening to burst out, along with the unfiltered truth about Will, the flashes, Cecil's coat, and the box hidden in her kitchen cabinet. But she couldn't bring herself to tell Thomas any of it. He was offering to endure a lifetime of his own heartache just to be with her. She didn't even know what was in the box in her kitchen, but if he was willing to do that for her, she needed to open it before she came clean to him about everything. She wanted to have as many answers as she could before she revealed everything she'd learned. Thomas deserved to be able to make an informed decision about whether he wanted to be with her or not. In this moment, she just wanted to stop hurting him.

"I forgive you," she whispered.

"So does this mean you're my fiancée again?"

Evelyn couldn't commit yet. Not until she opened the box and found out what secrets it held. She let a few cumbersome moments pass before she clarified and hoped she wasn't being too hard on him. "Things are complicated right now. Can we wait a little while and see how things go with the flashes before we make that official?"

His entire frame sagged a bit at her answer, but he put on a brave face. "Of course. I understand."

He leaned forward and hugged her, relieved they were at least back in each other's good graces. "I'll be better. You'll see."

She squeezed her eyes to keep the tears from spilling out as she rested her chin on his shoulder, still locked in his embrace. "I know."

Chapter 21
2006

Will couldn't break free from the shock of what he'd just heard. He was still in Caroline Huber's living room, trying to make sense of what she had told him. "You *knew* Evelyn in the other timeline? Personally?"

Caroline's mouth curled into a nostalgic smile. "I did. She was just a child then."

"How did you know each other?"

"We were in the dreamer studies together. She wouldn't remember me, of course. I was much younger and much prettier then." She stopped to grin at her own joke. "And Evelyn was still a very small girl. I think she was barely four years old when they took her out of the studies."

Will blinked as he hurriedly processed the information. "Wait, you're telling me Fletcher and Holstead did dreamer research on Evelyn when she was a kid?"

Caroline shook her head. "Not Doctor Holstead. He didn't come along until later. Evelyn had already left."

"Left? Where did she go? Why did they take her out of the studies?" He realized he was firing off questions and took a breath to gather himself. "I'm sorry, this is just a lot to take in."

"I understand," Caroline said, putting her coffee cup down on the table. "I don't know where Evelyn went after she left the studies. I was told she had been dismissed but never found out why. I assumed her parents had yanked her out." Her hands were now clasped into a tight ball.

"You said Evelyn was the most powerful dreamer you saw."

"She was. The rest of us paled in comparison. She could do things we couldn't."

"Like what?"

Caroline shifted in her seat. "I remember there was a time Doctor Fletcher spent a few weeks trying to figure out if we could bring things with us when we traveled between timelines. Physical objects. A group of us tried for days on end. We were exhausted from all Fletcher put us through trying to get it to work, but in the end only Evelyn succeeded."

Will furrowed his brow. He'd never thought of the possibility that a dreamer could transport a physical item between timelines. "What did she bring to that timeline with her?"

"A doll. It had a little yellow dress. I remember her holding it tightly to her chest as she walked into the lab."

Will rubbed his hands over his face, overwhelmed with the new knowledge about Caroline's connection to Evelyn. He was amazed that they'd been so close to learning all this at the church in 2003. He wished he'd tried harder to talk to Caroline more that day. "So you've experienced the flashes—or the daydreams—too? How often does it happen?"

Caroline hesitated before finally answering. "Well, I prefer not to let it happen much if I can help it. If I stay away from the triggers, I don't have the daydreams. But I didn't have as much to go back to in my other life, and I didn't have the stamina Evelyn does. I'd be willing to bet she could withstand more daydreams than any of us." She looked down at her feet thoughtfully, as though she was contemplating how much to tell Will. "You just have to remember she'll need time between visits to recover physically before she can do it again. It's draining in many ways."

Will was quiet for a few moments. "I just want to see her again."

Caroline leaned forward and put her hand on his knee to comfort him. "Unfortunately, this is the curse of the daydreams. Waiting every second for the dreamer to return, unsure of what you'll be doing when they pop up. It's part of the reason I don't like to flash back, as you call it. I wouldn't want the few people I cared about in my other timeline to spend their lives waiting for my visits. I wanted them to live for themselves and truly move forward."

"So you never showed yourself to them?"

"No." Caroline's eyes now stared past her feet at the rug on the floor, though she might as well have been gazing right through it down to the core of the earth. "I couldn't put them through it."

"Do you think Evelyn is selfish for showing herself to me? That this will end badly?"

Caroline finally lifted her eyes. "Not selfish, no. I imagine if I had the love of two lifetimes to fight for and my whole life ahead of me like Evelyn does, I might have handled my daydreams differently."

"And how do you think this will end for us?"

She sighed and crinkled her forehead. "I can't tell you that. But if Evelyn is as determined to see you as she was to bring that doll with her into that timeline when she was a toddler, I can assure you it won't be long before you find out."

Half an hour later, Will was on his way back to the city. As he drove, he couldn't stop replaying everything Caroline had told him that day. Evelyn had no idea she'd been part of the dreamer studies. If she had known, she surely would have told him about it. If everything Caroline had said was right, then Evelyn had probably been taken out of the studies before she was old enough to remember much. Something about the story was leaving a sick feeling in his stomach. It wasn't adding up. And something about Caroline's body language was bothering him, too. It was as if she was still keeping something about the daydreams from him.

He wished he could somehow get to Evelyn in her other timeline and tell her about his meeting with Caroline. For the time being, there was nothing he could do but wait for Evelyn to daydream her way back into his life again.

Chapter 22

1922

Evelyn closed the door behind Thomas after they said goodnight. She was glad they'd made up and that they'd agreed on holding off their engagement until everything settled down, but she was also relieved he was gone. She hated to rush him out, but she became increasingly impatient to find out what was in the box Mariah had given her.

She locked the door and waited a few minutes to make sure Thomas didn't come back for any reason and then retrieved the box from the kitchen cabinet. Back in the living room, she finally sat down and lifted the lid. Setting it aside, she leaned forward and peered inside the box. She'd expected paperwork. Research. Science. Whatever it was, Evelyn had no doubt it was going to change everything.

One by one, Evelyn took each object from the box and examined it.

A silver baby rattle engraved with initials. "E.C.F.," she whispered aloud to herself as she traced the initials with her fingertip.

Next was a small doll with a face and hands of pale bisque, wearing a yellow dress.

She reached into the box again and lifted out an old photograph. The edges were worn and fold marks crisscrossed the picture from edge to edge, but Evelyn could clearly see a young girl with blonde curls, maybe around age three, standing with her parents. When she looked closer, Evelyn realized the woman in the photo was a younger Mariah. She had been much more vibrant then, Evelyn noticed as she gazed at the lively eyes of the youthful mother in the photo. Evelyn wondered what had happened to Mrs. Fletcher's daughter. Mariah hadn't mentioned having a child when they'd talked. She assumed the man was Doctor Fletcher. She'd never seen a picture of him before. He was tall with a full beard and prominent brow. She'd envisioned him differently in her mind.

The last item in the box was an unmarked envelope. Evelyn turned it over and lifted the flap. She slid out two pieces of paper. She placed the smaller of the two next to her and flipped the other right side up so she could read it. The Fletcher family tree depicted several generations of Doctor Fletcher's lineage. His mother's name, Agatha Fletcher (née Prescott), was circled in red and labeled "O.D." for some reason. Not stopping to decode the initials, she followed the tree down. It ended with "Baby Girl Fletcher" who had been born in 1901. Evelyn's heart broke for Mariah as she put together that the Fletcher's had a baby born the same year she'd been born. It was impossible not to ponder what fate had befallen the Fletchers' child. It probably wasn't good, if Mariah never spoke about it. She put the family tree down on the couch and picked up the second piece of paper. It was a birth certificate from the State of New York. When she read further, she drew a sharp breath and covered her mouth, astonished.

Right there, in black and white, was an official birth document that stated baby girl Evelyn Claire had been born in 1901, in New York City, to Doctor and Mrs. Harold Fletcher.

"E.C.F.," Evelyn whispered to herself again as she stared at the rattle on the table in front of her and the birth certificate in her hand. "Evelyn Claire Fletcher."

The shock of her new reality cemented her to the couch. Everything she'd ever known about her life was a lie. Her entire life scrolled through her head at once, and her pulse quickened as she came to grips with the enormity of the truth. Evelyn put the birth certificate down and leaned back. She closed her eyes and breathed deeply, trying to calm herself. She held it for a few seconds before slowly exhaling and repeated the exercise a few more times before the panic began to subside. Thomas had taught her this coping mechanism, as he called it, the night they'd first met just after she'd been mugged. She wished he hadn't left now. She could use his strong, steady nature and take-charge instincts. The last few days had been a whirlwind of life-altering discoveries, and this one was an absolute bombshell. She was in no position to think clearly. In fact, she wished she could not think at all.

Choosing to pour herself a drink, which she rarely did on her own, she reached into the very back of a kitchen cabinet and pulled out a well-hidden bottle. Only she and Thomas knew about it because of prohibition laws, but she kept it around for a rainy day. And this was nothing if not a rainy day. She insisted on keeping the liquor hidden even though she couldn't imagine anyone she knew ratting her out to law enforcement. It just comforted her to know it was tucked away as their little secret. Evelyn poured herself a glass of the stiff liquid before putting the bottle back into hiding. She threw the drink down her throat and rinsed out her glass, leaving it to dry next to the sink. Once she was finally in bed, she squeezed her eyes shut and tried in vain not to cry until she fell into a fitful sleep.

Chapter 23

1922

Evelyn woke up with her eyes stinging and a pounding headache. After a few moments of confusion, she recollected the night before, and her stomach twisted itself into an instant knot. She climbed out of bed. Parched, she chugged a glass of water before washing her face, brushing her teeth, and re-applying her makeup. She dressed quickly, and in spite of feeling a bit groggy from all the sobbing and the stiff drink she'd had before bed, she hurried down to the lobby and out onto the busy city sidewalk. The sunlight was harsh on her eyes, which were dry from all the crying. In moments like this she missed the small conveniences of her other timeline, like mass-produced sunglasses, which she knew wouldn't exist in this timeline until 1929. Only some famous film stars had sunglasses now. Shading her eyes with her hand, she hailed a taxi and gave the driver an address.

Soon, the car pulled up outside a boarded-up storefront on an up-and-coming block of 23rd Street. Evelyn paid the driver, got out, and approached the unmarked door. As she opened it, a bell attached to it rang, jarring her.

She looked around and saw no one. The place looked very different from the last time she'd been there. "Hello?"

The sound of shuffling came from somewhere in the building. After a few seconds, Thomas entered the room, dressed in dusty overalls splattered with paint. His jaw was set tightly as he rounded the corner, but his face lit up when he saw her.

"Oh, it's you! What a wonderful surprise!" he exclaimed. He approached her and carefully kissed her on the cheek, trying not to get wet paint on her clothing. "You hardly ever come here, let alone on a Sunday! What's the occasion?" As he talked, he hurriedly closed some ledgers and shuffled some paperwork from the desk into a drawer, crumpling some of them as he did.

Evelyn cocked her head, confused. "I won't keep you if you're busy."

Thomas returned to her side. "You're not keeping me!" He put his arm around her and pulled her in for a sideways hug. Evelyn thought it was a bit strange but wrote it off as him trying to avoid getting her clothes dirty with his dusty overalls.

"The office is really coming along." There was still much work to be done, but Evelyn could see past the furniture draped in protective sheets and the plaster shavings on the floor and admired how much progress Thomas and Karl had made in just a few weeks since she'd last seen the place.

"We've been working hard." He grunted as he lifted himself up to sit on the large wooden desk near the front door. He patted the spot next to him, urging her to join him. She walked over slowly and leaned back against the edge of the desk beside him.

"What's the matter?" Thomas asked, squinting at her to decipher her mood. He reached his arm around her shoulder again. "I can tell something's on your mind. Are you all right?"

Evelyn stood up straight and turned to face him.

Ignoring the dust and paint, he pulled her close to him and held her. "It's fine. Whatever it is, we'll get through it together. Just tell me."

She pulled back and sniffed, reaching into her bag for something. Silent, she held out an envelope. He took out the contents and scanned the family tree, then perused the birth certificate. His brows rose in a surprised arc when he recognized the massive implications of the small piece of paper he was holding. He looked up at her, wide-eyed and speechless.

"I found out last night," she said with a sudden sob, unable to hold back the emotional avalanche any longer. "My parents aren't my parents, Thomas!" She fell into his arms, her body heaving as she bawled into his chest. He held her and let her cry for as long as she needed. She eventually pulled back, having expended all her tears for the moment. Quietly, he handed her a handkerchief and waited for her to continue speaking.

"Why would a parent just give up their child? How could Mariah do that? How could *any* mother let her child go to someone else and never have any contact with them again? And how could she sit in the same room with me and not tell me?" She was out of breath and shaking.

"Okay, let's slow down." Thomas put the birth certificate on the desk and took both her hands, squeezing them. "This is a lot of shocking information for anyone to process at once. Let's take it one step at a time."

He let go and began stripping off his overalls.

"What are you doing?"

"Well, we're not going to figure out your life-changing discovery here in the middle of a construction zone. I'm taking you to my house for dinner."

They soon arrived at the large Manhattan brownstone where Thomas lived with his mother, Nancy. The plan was for him to remain there until he and Evelyn were married, at which time they would move in together. Nancy was always thrilled when Thomas brought Evelyn over, and today was no exception. She sent Thomas off to talk to the cook about dinner and took the opportunity to catch up with Evelyn.

"How are you, dear?" She smiled warmly as she guided Evelyn into the sitting room. "Have you had any luck finding an apartment?"

They sat facing each other, and Evelyn smoothed her skirt, trying to appear as unfazed as possible in spite of the life-altering information she was grappling with at the moment. "No, nothing yet."

"This city!" Nancy huffed. "It's getting so crowded these days. It's a wonder there are any empty apartments at all!"

Evelyn stifled a chuckle thinking about how much more crowded New York would become in just a few decades. If only Nancy

Allen could see Manhattan in 2006. The thought amused her, which was a welcome relief from the endless parade of questions and emotions that had been consuming her since the moment she'd opened that box the night before.

"Anyway," Nancy continued, "I'm sure you'll find something soon. In the meantime, I'm not in a rush to have Thomas leave me or for your visits to become less frequent."

"You have nothing to worry about. We'll come and visit all the time, no matter where we're living. I promise." Evelyn meant it. If she and Thomas made it that long.

"That means so much to me. I know you'll get busier when you're married. Especially when you start growing your family." Nancy raised her eyebrows as she said the last part. She always did when she talked about her desire to have grandchildren.

Evelyn managed a genuine laugh this time, surprising herself. "I think when I have children, I'll need you even more!" The moment of levity was short-lived as she remembered she and Thomas weren't even technically engaged at the moment, but Nancy didn't know that, and she didn't need to. Not yet. Evelyn needed to change the subject. "Thomas mentioned you'll be visiting the Hamptons soon. Are you looking forward to seeing your cousins?"

"Oh yes, very much. I'm sure they could use the company. They don't get out much these days, you know." Nancy rarely left Manhattan, but when she did, it was typically to go out east and visit her cousins, Ivy and Gwendolyn. They were both widowed and lived together in a large cottage along the beach in Quogue. Nancy described it as quaint and peaceful except in the summer months when the ferry carted loads of tourists into town for their vacations. Evelyn had always thought it sounded lovely and hoped she could visit someday. Nancy's voice snapped her out of her musings. "I don't suppose you and Thomas would have any free time to join me on this visit, would you?"

"Sadly, no. Thomas won't be able to leave the office that long, and I have appointments with some real estate brokers that we're hoping will lead us to the right place, finally."

"That's too bad. It would have been so nice to have you both along." She sighed and smiled at Evelyn. "You know, sometimes I think about what Thomas would be doing right now if you hadn't walked into his office that night and swept him off his feet. He was so wound up in his studies that I wondered if he'd ever find someone to share his life with. He certainly wouldn't have gone out looking for a wife."

Evelyn was surprised to hear Nancy speak so frankly but quietly agreed that Thomas may have never sought out romance of his own volition, and she wondered if they ever would have met if her boss hadn't sent her to his doorstep. Out loud, she said simply, "Thomas is a wonderful man. I'm sure someone would have snatched him up eventually."

They were interrupted when Thomas entered the room to let them know dinner would be ready soon. He glanced back and forth at the two women, sizing up whether Evelyn had shared her newest discovery with his mother.

Evelyn caught his gaze. "Now that you're back, we should share with your mother what I learned last night."

"What is it? Is everything all right?" Nancy stood up and clasped her hands in front of her, bracing for bad news.

"Yes, we're both fine," Evelyn assured her. "I just found out some rather unsettling news. It's about my parents."

"Are *they* all right?" Nancy was beginning to get worked up.

Evelyn jumped in to quell her fears. "They're quite well. It's nothing like that. Let's go in to dinner and we'll talk about it."

Over a dinner of beef stew, Thomas and Evelyn shared the upsetting information they'd learned about Evelyn's birth parents. Nancy put her fork down and covered her mouth upon hearing Evelyn's parents weren't who she thought they were. Nancy was aghast at the idea that Evelyn was dealing with such a monumental realization about her family. "Evelyn, I'm so sorry. This must all be devastating for you." She stood up from her dining chair and rounded the table to where Evelyn was sitting. Nancy bent down and hugged Evelyn from behind, surprising both Evelyn and Thomas. "You know I love you like a daughter. My heart breaks for you. But you will be fine, I promise." She straightened up and walked back to her chair. "If there is anything I can do for you, please just say the word." She sat.

Evelyn nodded, silent, and looked at her dinner plate.

Thomas interjected. "All we can do is be supportive, Mother. We'll let Evelyn take the lead."

Mrs. Allen nodded in agreement and the three sat in an uncomfortable silence for several minutes.

"Are you full?" Nancy asked them both, unsure of what else to do. "Shall I have Irina prepare anything more?"

"Perhaps some coffee and tea," Thomas said. Nancy left the room and Thomas turned to Evelyn, taking her hand.

"You're going to be fine, you know. This doesn't change anything. You're still you."

She scoffed. "That's just the problem, isn't it? Being me wasn't enough for the Fletchers. Something about being *me* made them give me away."

"I doubt that's how it happened. There must be more to it than that."

"What possible reason could be good enough to abandon your own child? And I'm a dreamer! Wasn't that all Fletcher cared about? Why wouldn't he want me if I could help him with his research?"

He shook his head slowly. "I don't know. But I would put money on the fact that it wasn't anything to do with you being you."

She looked at him, her eyes bloodshot from crying so much that day. "What else do I not know? What more have they kept from me all this time?"

"Do you think Holstead knows anything about this?" Thomas asked.

"No. I can't imagine he does. He said he partnered with Doctor Fletcher later on. I would have been gone already. And surely he would have told me if he'd known. Wouldn't he?" She was starting to get overwhelmed again as she contemplated the whole debacle, and her pulse began racing. She relaxed when Thomas lovingly used his thumb to wipe away a rogue tear that had escaped her eye.

"We'll start finding your answers tomorrow," he said. "Tonight, I'm going to take care of you. You can stay the night in the extra bedroom."

She leaned over and rested her head on his shoulder. In the back of her mind, overshadowed by the shattering discovery she'd just made, was the fact that she still hadn't been completely honest with Thomas about her flashes and her conversation with Will. She promised herself she would tell him when the time was right.

Tonight, she needed his reassuring presence.

Chapter 24
2006

It had been a long day at work for Will. He hadn't been able to get Caroline's words out of his head. *The most powerful dreamer I ever saw.* When the sun finally began to set, Will wrapped up one last email, said goodbye to Jamie, and left the office. As soon as he opened the main doors of the building, a brisk burst of air reminded him it was starting to get cold. He contemplated going back up to his office to retrieve a hoodie he kept there for when it got chilly, but before he could decide, he caught sight of Caroline Huber walking toward him.

"Caroline?" Will squinted, confused. "What are you doing here?"

"There's more about the daydreams you should know. I should have told you yesterday."

He bit his lip, perplexed. "What is it?"

"Is there somewhere we can sit? I've been waiting a while on the edge of this planter for you to come out." She smiled, gesturing to the uncomfortable marble flower bed behind her.

He nodded. "I know a place."

Minutes later, Will and Caroline were seated on a bench alongside a small park in the rear of the UN building. The only people who ever visited were those who worked in the building. It was a tiny patch of green that housed a few beds with flowers that bloomed in the warmer months. The singular bench was about as private a spot as one could hope for in one of the most crowded cities in the world.

"I'm sorry I didn't tell you everything at my place," she began. "It's just—I saw how happy you were when I told you Evelyn would visit again that I didn't have the heart to take that joy away from you."

"Is Evelyn in danger?" His brow furrowed in concern.

"No," Caroline answered. "Well, not exactly. Not yet."

Will stared at her, urging her to go on.

"When dreamers daydream—or flash, as you said—to their former timelines, it takes a toll on their bodies."

"Yes, you mentioned that yesterday."

Caroline continued. "What I failed to mention is that the more daydreams one has, and the longer each daydream is, the worse the *permanent* effects will be on the dreamer."

Will looked out at the East River in front of them and considered her words carefully before responding. "So, you're telling me that by visiting me, Evelyn is harming herself forever?"

"Yes. And she may not know it. But I know what too much daydreaming can do to a person, and I wouldn't want that for Evelyn. Or for you."

"Is there any way to repair the damage done? If she waits a while between visits, will she be strong enough to do it again safely the next time?" He was afraid to hear the answer.

"Sadly, no. None that I'm aware of. It's almost like a battery draining. After I lost my other timeline, I felt an energy about me. Something that still tugged at me from the other life. The first time I daydreamed, I came back and noticed that energy—that buzz—had waned. It was only slightly, but it was enough for me to feel it. I thought maybe I was just tired. But days passed and the energy didn't recharge. The next time I flashed back, I came back feeling less of the energy again."

Caroline paused to give Will a chance to speak or ask questions. He said nothing but stared at the water behind her, the wheels in his head turning a million miles an hour as he put together what it all meant for Evelyn. Since he didn't stop her, Caroline kept talking.

"If Evelyn isn't careful, she will lose the ability to visit. The energy will be lost, and it can't be regained. And she can't come here too often or stay too long. If she does, she risks her well-being in her own timeline. Evelyn is a powerful dreamer, like I said, but everyone has their limit."

Will sat back and stared directly ahead of him at the side of a building. He let out a long, exasperated sigh. "So I'm going to lose her again? Is that what you're telling me?" He scoffed. "Of course. Of *course* I'll lose her again!" He stood up. Anger rose in him as he walked away from the bench with his hands clasped behind his head. He stopped and stood still for a few moments before finally turning around to speak.

"I need to talk to Evelyn. Please, Caroline. Help me find a way to get to 1922."

Chapter 25

1922

The early morning hours were upon her, but Evelyn still hadn't been able to fall asleep. The guest room at Thomas's house was cozy and comfortable, but no matter how she tried to stop it, her mind spun relentlessly.

She climbed out of bed and walked to the window, sure to keep her footsteps light so she didn't disturb Thomas or Nancy. As she pulled the curtain aside and peered out onto the city street, she almost wished she hadn't taken Thomas up on his offer to spend the night. She had felt much better before he'd gone to bed, but since then, she'd spent hours alone with her thoughts. In spite of Thomas's and Nancy's hospitality, Evelyn couldn't help wishing she were home in her apartment. She wanted nothing more than to wrap Cecil's coat around her shoulders again and visit Will so she could tell him what was happening in her timeline. He always knew what to say or do to make her feel better.

As the moon cast a bright glow over the dimly lit street below, Evelyn pictured the same street in her other timeline and how much it would change over the decades. The streetlights, which were still a modern marvel to many in this life, would be replaced over time by much brighter, more powerful ones. The cars, still quaint and relatively slow, would eventually become the sleek, more automated ones of the future. And yet, she observed, many of the buildings remained the same. She'd always thought it fascinating in her other life how the architecture closer to the ground screamed of the old days, while that above it gleamed with modernity. In Manhattan, there was nowhere to build but up, but the foundation of the city was rooted in exactly where Evelyn now stood.

Lost in thought, her heart skipped a beat when a woman's voice from behind her spoke softly. "Evelyn, please don't be afraid. It's me, Caroline."

Evelyn's legs almost fell out from under her. Once she had taken a few moments to calm down from the initial shock of Caroline Huber appearing in her room out of nowhere, Evelyn sat on the edge of the bed and collected her thoughts. She never thought she would see Caroline again and couldn't fathom how she was here, or why.

"I know my coming here like this is a surprise," Caroline said, now standing near the window where Evelyn had been. "But I have a message for you. From Will. He wanted to come here himself, but this was the next best thing."

Evelyn's pulse sped up at the very mention of Will's name. "What does he need to tell me?"

"He wanted you to know that he understands if you can't visit him anymore. If it gets too hard for you. He doesn't want you to hurt yourself."

The idea of never seeing Will again was not one Evelyn was willing to accept. She'd only just gotten him back. She gripped her nightgown at her sides to prepare for whatever Caroline was about to tell her. "Why would it be too hard?"

Caroline explained what she'd told Will about the daydreams and about their effect on the dreamer who visited another timeline. She was careful to reiterate that a dreamer only had so many visits in them and that Evelyn should use them wisely, if at all. As she talked, Evelyn's shoulders dropped, and her eyes filled with sadness.

"I don't mean to be the bearer of bad news," Caroline said regretfully. "But Will came to me for help, and we both wanted you to know that the visits to our timeline can be dangerous for you." Evelyn was silent, so Caroline carried on. "I know how hard it is to have a love torn away from you by the dreams. I wish I had better news for you. I'm sorry."

"How did you get here?"

"The same way you got to Will. I held the letter you wrote him before you died."

"If the flashes—daydreams—are so dangerous, why would you risk coming here to tell me this? Why risk it for someone you barely know?"

A faraway smile came over Caroline's face. "But I do know you."

"I don't understand."

"You won't remember me," Caroline replied, "but we knew each other when you were just a very small child. You couldn't have been more than three or four when we parted ways."

Evelyn tried to piece things together in her head. "Did you meet me when Doctor Fletcher was studying you?" She almost wanted to blurt out that Fletcher was actually her father, but she hadn't even finished processing that part mentally let alone come to terms with it enough to say it out loud in conversation with anyone but Thomas.

"Yes," Caroline said. "How could I forget? You were the star of his studies."

Her words were a punch to Evelyn's gut. "His studies?" She felt her pulse begin to race. "He studied *me*?"

"I'm sorry," Caroline said, clapping her hand over her mouth. "I assumed you already knew, since you'd been digging up information about the dreams for so long. I didn't mean to—"

"So he studied me until I was three or four and then he sent me away?" Evelyn sneered. "What kind of monster does that?" She was pacing now, too distracted to bother softening her footsteps.

Unsure of what Evelyn meant, Caroline stayed silent, allowing the young woman's audible thought process to play out. Eventually, Evelyn turned to her. "What did I do wrong?"

Caroline tilted her head, confused. "What do you mean?"

"To get sent away. What did I do that was so horrible they had to send me away?"

"I always assumed your parents were the ones who took you from the studies?"

Evelyn tilted her head toward the ceiling and took a deep breath before exhaling and explaining to Caroline what she'd learned about the Fletchers being her birth parents.

Caroline was flabbergasted. "I had no idea," she whispered. "He never mentioned it. Never treated you any differently than the rest of us. When did you find out?"

"Two days ago, actually." Evelyn's voice was shaking. Caroline walked toward Evelyn and wrapped her arms around her.

"I'm so sorry. That must be a terrible shock."

"It is," Evelyn said, returning Caroline's embrace. "And now to find out my own father used me as a research participant. It's all too much."

Caroline let go of Evelyn and sat back on the edge of the bed. "If it's any consolation, Mrs. Fletcher—your mother—was always so caring and warm with you. None of us knew you were their daughter, obviously, but it was always so sweet to watch her with you when you came in. We all thought she just had a soft spot for you."

Evelyn relaxed a little. "It helps a bit, I suppose. Although it makes me wonder what kind of life I could have had with her as my mother if she was so loving and sweet."

"May I ask you something?"

Evelyn nodded.

"Did you have a good life with your parents? The ones who adopted you?"

"Yes."

"Then don't worry about the life you didn't have. Especially now that you have a chance to have a relationship with your birth mother in addition to a wonderful set of parents who raised you and care about you more than anything."

Evelyn blinked slowly. Caroline was right. She now had an opportunity to have both her mothers in her life as well as a father who had given her everything. She was grateful to have Caroline's perspective, even if her visit had been most unexpected.

"I hope I've helped and not hurt you more," Caroline said. "I can't stay much longer."

"I understand. And you've helped more than you know. Can I send a message back with you? For Will?"

"Of course."

"Tell him I'll see him again *very* soon. And that I don't care how dangerous it is."

Chapter 26

1922

Evelyn was fuming when she finally arrived on Mariah Fletcher's front step the next morning. She'd spent all night simmering over the many secrets the Fletchers and the Moores had kept from her. She banged loudly on the door, and when it opened, Mariah gave her a sheepish smile. "I'm so glad you—"

Evelyn pushed past Mariah and barged into the house, stopping halfway to the sitting room to face the woman she now knew was her birth mother. "Well?" she asked sharply. "Don't you have some things you'd like to tell me?"

Mariah's face went pale. She nodded shamefacedly and walked past Evelyn into the sitting room. She remained silent. Evelyn couldn't imagine what she could possibly say that would make it better, anyway.

Mariah sat across from Evelyn, her hands nervously folded in her lap. Finally, after what seemed like an endless silence, Evelyn looked her in the eye and spoke. "Why didn't you want me?"

A sudden sob erupted from Mariah. After she'd gathered herself, she looked at Evelyn through wide, teary eyes. "Is that what you think? That I didn't want you?"

Evelyn simply stared at her, waiting for an answer.

"I have never loved anything or anyone as much as I loved you. I still do. All I ever wanted was you."

Evelyn's own eyes were beginning to sting with tears. She didn't want to cry. Not yet. "I don't understand! Who are they? The Moores? Why did you send me away to them? What did I do that was so bad?" The tears had already won out.

"It was to protect you! I promise it was all to keep you safe!" Mariah stood. Her emotions were too big for an armchair to contain. She walked over to Evelyn and reached down to fondly fix a stray wisp of hair from her daughter's hairdo. Evelyn stiffened at her touch. Mariah withdrew her hand and walked over to the window, peering out of it as she spoke.

"You were a surprise, you know. We weren't expecting to have children at all. It wasn't part of our plan. But the moment I found out about you, I fell in love. It was the best thing that had ever happened to me."

Evelyn swallowed but said nothing, prompting Mariah to go on.

"The first year was pure bliss. You were such a happy baby. Always babbling away, and you slept so soundly. We went for long walks around the city with you in the baby carriage and you would stare wide-eyed at the buildings and the trees.

"Things changed around the time you began talking. It quickly became clear that your sound sleep was not just luck on our part, and Fletch soon caught on that you were a dreamer. Imagine his delight; the thing he was most interested in studying had appeared in his very own family! For some reason he was always convinced it would. He immediately wanted to examine you and put you through tests and do research on you like all his other dreamers, but I put up a fight. I didn't want you to go through all that so young. And it would take you away from me for hours each day. I would miss precious time with you that I couldn't get back, and I was angry with Fletch for suggesting it."

Mariah turned back to Evelyn, who was rooted to her seat, staring at the carpet but listening intently to every word. "Fletch got his way most of the time, though some days I convinced him to let you stay with me while he worked with the other dreamers. They were all much older than you. They could decide whether they wanted to be studied. It felt wrong for me to subject you to it all when you had no say, but Fletcher was a man, and he was a doctor. As a woman, my opinion may as well have been a whisper in the wind.

"Our marriage became very strained, the main source of conflict being his insistence on studying you. As you got a little older, you started to show signs of what he said made you the most significant dreamer he'd ever studied. I never knew exactly what that meant, but the more he found out about your abilities, the more crazed he became about studying them. I often wondered if he had somehow been affected by a dreamer in his childhood and maybe that's what made him so obsessed with studying it, but I never said anything, and he never mentioned it. We barely talked at all during that time because I hated him for using you like a lab rat. It was like he'd lost all sense of fatherhood. I was disgusted."

"Is that when I knew Caroline?"

Surprised at the interruption and the question itself, Mariah cocked her head, indicating she hadn't heard correctly. "Caroline?"

"Caroline Huber. She was a dreamer in the studies. She said she knew me back then."

"Yes, I remember her. She was always so sweet with you. I think she felt the same way I did about Fletch studying you."

"She said I disappeared from the studies one day after I was able to bring my doll with me from that timeline into this one. Why?"

"Ah. That was the proverbial straw that broke the camel's back. Fletch and I had been going at it for almost two years about him including you in his research. My patience was wearing thin, and the more he learned about your abilities, the more determined he became. He started going behind my back, sending me on fool's errands so he could relieve the nanny for the day and take you into the lab. One day I came home and you were nowhere to be found, so naturally I rushed over to his lab to ask him if he'd seen you. What I found was a mother's worst nightmare. I didn't find out until later that he'd forced you to transport your favorite doll across timelines.

"There you were, lying on a gurney, convulsing, shaking, foaming at the mouth. Fletch was desperately trying to revive you. I didn't know exactly what he'd done to cause it, but the second you came out of it, I scooped you up and dashed out of the lab. I ran to a friend's house down the block and we hid from Fletch for hours. When I finally went back home, I left you with my friends to be safe. Fletch was furious with me, and I with him. We fought for hours. He absolutely refused to give up studying you, even though I could see it was hurting you. Finally, I gave him an ultimatum. I told him that if he didn't stop, I would leave him and take you with me. He would never see us again."

Evelyn stared at Mariah, her eyes wide.

"You see, divorce was a massive scandal back then. Much more so than it is now. If I had left him and taken his child, it would have destroyed Fletch's reputation in the medical field and in this city. He would have had to give up the dreamer studies and move away. I knew he would never sacrifice his life's work. It was a gamble on my part, assuming he wouldn't call my bluff." Mariah was pacing the room as she spoke. "The problem was it was all talk. I couldn't leave. I had nowhere to go. No family to turn to. When I met Fletcher, I had nothing, and if I left, I would have even less than I started with. I wouldn't be able to take care of myself, let alone you, and I didn't want that life for you." She stopped pacing and faced Evelyn directly, her eyes wide as decades of secrets tumbled out of her. "You deserved so much better. So finally I agreed to let you go and live with other parents where Fletch couldn't get to you, so you'd be safe from the experiments and whatever they were doing to you, and I wouldn't have to be destitute for the rest of my miserable life. Fletcher only agreed to it on the condition that the adoptive parents would keep him up to date on your health and any developments with your dreams." She took a moment to collect herself. This part of the story was clearly difficult for her to relive. "We went through an adoption agency here in the city. They knew of a couple in Virginia who was desperate for a child but hadn't been able to have any of their own. I met with the Moores, and I must have asked them a million and one questions. As much as it broke every piece of me, I knew they were the ones. I trusted them."

"So they just . . . took me away?"

"The day I had to watch that train pull away with you inside it was—and still is—the worst day of my entire life. I know it's not much consolation to you now, but after that day I didn't get out of bed for months. I was a wreck. I couldn't eat or sleep. I had no desire to do anything at all. I was a ghost of myself. I blamed Fletcher for all of it and our marriage was never the same until the day he died. *I've* never been the same."

Evelyn was wiping tears off her cheeks as she listened.

"The arrangement was that the Moores were never to tell you about us or the dreamers. That if you ever brought up the dreams to them, they were to minimize it the best they could so you wouldn't seek out more information and wind up in the studies again."

"So they've known this entire time that I was a dreamer?" Evelyn asked, incredulous. "My entire life everyone has been lying to me?"

"No, dear," Mariah corrected her. "Not lying. Protecting you. It's all I ever wanted. All the Moores wanted. I kept in touch with them through the years. They sent me letters and photographs. Told me all about you and how well you did with your schooling. When they wrote and told me you were moving to New York to go to secretarial school a few years back, I was elated. I thought perhaps with Fletch gone this would be my chance to reconnect with you somehow. Have you back in my life. But I knew it would only complicate things for you and I wanted you to keep living your successful, happy life. One without the dreamer research overshadowing it." She began to cry again. "So I stayed away and didn't try to find you. It's been crushing my soul ever since, knowing you're so close by. And the other day, when you showed up on my doorstep with Walter, I knew in an instant it was you. I wanted to cry, wrap you in my arms, tell you how much I'd missed you and wished for you to come back." She paused. She was now weeping too hard to keep talking.

Evelyn slowly stood up from her chair and walked to where Mariah was standing, facing her. She pulled out a handkerchief and gently dabbed the older woman's face with it. The moment of tenderness conveyed a silent forgiveness Mariah must have been praying for since Evelyn left her as a child. The women simply looked at each other and fell into an embrace that left them both sobbing in each other's arms.

"I'm sorry," Mariah said between tears. "I'm so, so sorry. I've missed you so much!"

The two stayed locked in their emotional hug for a long while until they had both exhausted all their tears. When they let go and gathered themselves, Evelyn had a sudden thought.

"Can I ask you something?"

"Anything," Mariah said, wiping her eyes.

"What was the combination on the safe behind the painting?"

A nostalgic and slightly mischievous smile spread across Mariah's face. "Your birthday, of course."

Chapter 27
1922

A bouquet of flowers in hand, Thomas headed directly to Evelyn's apartment after he finished working at the office. He had begged her to wait a day so he could go with her to Mariah Fletcher's house. Understandably, Evelyn had refused. She wanted answers as quickly as she could get them, and Thomas couldn't blame her.

Since they were back on good terms, he used his key to enter the apartment. He had been distracted all day thinking about Evelyn's meeting with Mariah and what life-changing things she might learn. He was concerned for her, and he couldn't imagine what she was going through but intended to be there for her no matter what.

The living room and kitchen were empty. Thomas carefully placed the flowers on the counter and crept into the bedroom, where he found Evelyn fast asleep on the bed, fully clothed. He watched for a moment to confirm she was all right. Once he was satisfied she was simply exhausted, he drew the curtains closed. He pulled the blanket over her and gently removed the tear-stained handkerchief from her fist. He stood for a while, staring at her. Guilt ate at Thomas for going to work instead of accompanying her to Mariah's. He was beginning to realize Evelyn's gripes about his work hours and lack of personal time were more legitimate than he'd given them credit for. He wanted to be more present and helpful to her, but he was working himself to the limit to get his practice up and running to secure their future as a couple. As a family. And, though he hadn't yet shared it with Evelyn, there was more to his business dealings than he'd let on.

He had been keeping it all close to his chest, not only to protect her, but also because he felt like a complete idiot. He'd made some poor business decisions and become wrapped up with a deal on the new office that had ultimately put his family home on the line. His mother had no idea any of it was happening, and Thomas was saddled with worry every moment that if he didn't get things right, Nancy would be put out of her house, humiliated. He didn't even want to know what Evelyn would think of him. He never wanted to disappoint her, but he'd gotten in over his head, and now their entire future was in jeopardy because of it. Hiding everything from his fiancée had been tormenting him for weeks. He was trying every avenue before he gave in and came clean, but Thomas knew his options were running out, and he needed to tell Evelyn what was going on sooner rather than later. He simply hadn't been able to bring it up while she was going through all this turmoil with her family and the flashes.

He took one last, loving look at her before he padded out of the bedroom and clicked the door shut. As he did his best to arrange the flowers he'd brought in a vase of water, he pondered all the ways Evelyn's conversation with Mariah could have gone. He was worried about what all this new information would do to her. She had been so fragile after losing her other timeline and had worked so hard to get to a better place since. He would hate to see it all undone.

He decided to stay the night, assuming Evelyn might not want to be alone if she woke up. He quietly popped out of the apartment and went down to the lobby to inform Edward that he would be staying over on Evelyn's sofa to take care of her because she was feeling unwell. Edward asked no questions. He had become fond of Evelyn over the years, and he was happy to know Thomas would be there to watch over her if she wasn't feeling up to par. He told Thomas to let him know if there was anything he could do to help, and Thomas thanked him before taking the stairs back up to Evelyn's apartment. It wasn't any of Edward's business, really, but Thomas knew if he didn't clear things up, Evelyn would worry that people might get the wrong idea. They weren't yet married, after all.

He locked the door behind him and quietly went into the bedroom to check on Evelyn again. Back in the living room, he shut the curtains. He draped a throw blanket over himself on the sofa and read over some work documents until his eyelids grew heavy and he drifted off.

Chapter 28
2006

Will had been thinking about Caroline Huber all day while he was at work. He was worried about her. When she'd come back from her daydream in the park behind the UN building, she seemed highly affected by the trip. It had taken her several minutes to stop shaking and come around enough to be able to form the words to tell Will that she'd delivered his message to Evelyn. Will was relieved that Evelyn now knew the dangers of visiting him, but he couldn't help feeling responsible that Caroline had been left so weak and unwell because she'd done him a favor.

He left work and took a train almost two hours to Saugerties. He grabbed a cab outside the train station and headed to Caroline's house. If he was being completely honest, he also hoped to ask more questions about her visit with Evelyn. He'd picked up bits and pieces the day before, but in her confused state he couldn't be sure she'd told him everything.

He knocked on the door of Caroline's house for the second time that week. He wasn't surprised when Lydia rolled her eyes upon seeing him on the doorstep. She'd been pretty irritated the day before when she'd come to pick Caroline up after her talk with Will and found her mother in such a fragile state.

"Not you again."

"I know, I'm sorry. I just wanted to make sure she was okay."

Lydia shook her head. "Look, I don't know what you want with my mother, but this dreamer nonsense has taken enough from us over the years. We don't need this right now."

Will had been prepared for Lydia to be annoyed when he got there, but he hadn't considered how much having a dreamer for a parent had affected Lydia's entire life. His remorse was piling up.

"I totally understand why you hate me," he said. "I would probably feel the same way." Lydia's shoulders dropped a bit, and so did her defenses. She was listening. He continued. "I've lost a lot to the dreams, too. I get it."

Lydia sighed, exasperated, and pushed the door open with her back, motioning for him to enter. "Come on."

Once inside, Lydia peeked into Caroline's room. "She's asleep. You wanna wait around for a bit? She'll probably be up soon. She's been fitful."

"I don't want to be a bother," Will said uncomfortably. He was probably the last person Lydia wanted to host while Caroline slept.

"It's fine." She handed him a glass of water. "You can use the time to tell me exactly what it is you're doing with my mother."

Will was suddenly in a mini panic. He wasn't sure how much Lydia knew about her mother's dreams or daydreams, and he didn't want to inadvertently expose anything. He was aware of how carefully dreamers guarded their secrets and the myriad reasons why. "I'm not sure

I'm at liberty to talk about all of it." He glanced at Lydia. "But I can tell you my part."

He proceeded to explain to Lydia that Evelyn was on the other side, in Caroline's old timeline, and that he had hoped Caroline could help him answer some questions about her experiences as a dreamer. He told Lydia it was because he wanted to know if Caroline's dreams had ever come back. He didn't like lying to her, but he didn't want to reveal to her that Caroline could flash back.

"That doesn't explain why she came back from your little talk yesterday in the city in such a terrible state," Lydia quipped.

Will knew he had to lie again. He hated lying. "I don't know what happened. I'm sorry."

She glared at him, as though calculating how much of what he said she could believe. Before she could respond, they were interrupted by Caroline's voice calling from the bedroom.

"Do I hear Will?"

Lydia shot him a look that Will read loud and clear. She didn't want him upsetting her mother. "Uh-huh. He stopped by to see how you were feeling!"

"Send him in, won't you?"

"Are you sure you're up for visitors?" Lydia called, eyeing Will intently.

"Oh, for heaven's sake, Lydia, send him in!"

Lydia stood to lead the way to the bedroom door. Before she allowed Will in, she whispered gruffly, "Do *not* upset her."

Will nodded. Lydia stepped aside to let him in, following closely behind. Caroline beamed when she saw him. "How thoughtful of you to come all this way to check on me." She sounded cheerful, but Will couldn't ignore the weakness in her voice as she spoke.

Will walked over to the bedside and bent down to hug Caroline. "I'm sorry you're feeling so awful."

Caroline chuckled. "Oh, I'll be fine. Nothing a little rest can't fix, I'm sure. You be careful you don't catch this cold." She winked at him as she said it, out of Lydia's view. Will swallowed. He was keeping more secrets than he was used to, and he was growing increasingly uncomfortable. He reminded himself why he'd come in the first place. Evelyn was worth it. He wished Lydia weren't in the room so he could get the answers he sorely needed.

As if reading his mind, Caroline asked Lydia to fetch her a heating pad and a cup of tea. Lydia hesitantly left the room, giving Will a piercing look as she did.

Caroline wasted no time getting to the point. "I was too out of it yesterday to tell you everything, so I'll summarize quickly."

Will sat on a chair near the bed and leaned forward to hear everything. All she'd managed to tell him the day before was that she'd delivered his message to Evelyn. "Is she all right?" he asked, concerned.

"Yes." Caroline paused to rethink her answer. "Well, she's not in any danger, that is. But she's just found out some news that has upended her whole world."

The house phone rang, and they heard Lydia answer, giving them time to continue talking.

"She learned this week that Doctor Fletcher and his wife are her birth parents, and the people she's called her mother and father all her life are actually her adoptive parents."

Will's lips parted in shock. Evelyn would undoubtedly be crushed, and he longed to be there to comfort her.

Before he could ask any follow-up questions, Lydia reappeared in the doorway holding the house phone. "Mom, the pharmacy just called. They filled your prescription, but they close in forty-five minutes. Do you have enough to get you through until morning?"

Caroline reached over to her nightstand to check a pill bottle near the lamp. She shook it and it made no noise. "All out."

"I guess I need to get to the pharmacy." Lydia glanced at Will, obviously worried about leaving Caroline alone.

Will jumped at the opportunity to not only do a favor for them but also to get some real privacy so he and Caroline could talk candidly. "I'll stay with her if you want."

Lydia sighed loudly, stalling her departure as she looked from Will to Caroline and back. "Fine. But please be careful. Don't get her excited. No weird dream stuff?"

Will held up both hands. "Promise. I'm just here to help."

Lydia disappeared and soon Will and Caroline heard the sound of the front door clicking shut behind her as she left the house. Will didn't say anything, worried that she wasn't really gone or that he'd be blamed for upsetting Caroline somehow.

Caroline, however, did not appear worried. "Where were we?"

"Evelyn's birth parents," Will reminded her. "I can't believe it. How did she find out?"

"She said she'd been digging for information about her daydreams. She uncovered a bit more than she bargained for when she went to Doctor Fletcher's house to look for research."

"She must be devastated." He folded his arms across his chest.

"She is certainly in shock," Caroline confirmed. "But she's strong. Evelyn will be fine."

"Did she tell you anything else?"

Caroline smiled. "She says to tell you she's definitely coming back, no matter what."

Will shook his head, grinning slightly. He should have guessed she'd fight back. She'd always been fiery and ready for a challenge. His heart ached as he thought of how much he missed that part of her. "So much for warning her, I suppose." He laughed softly.

Caroline chuckled as well. "She's always been a little spitfire. Ever since she was this big." She held her hand out to indicate how small Evelyn had been when they'd known each other in the dreamer studies.

"There's something else." Will stopped fiddling with a framed photo on the dresser to listen as she continued. "I haven't even told Lydia yet, but I've had some news from my doctor. I'm afraid I might not have much longer."

Will turned to face her, his eyes wide. "What do you mean?"

"It's in my pancreas. And it's spreading. Quickly."

Will covered his eyes with his hands. "Caroline, I'm so sorry."

"Don't be. I've lived more life than most people could hope for. But there's one more thing I still need to do. And I need your help."

He walked to her bedside. "Name it."

She bit her lips thoughtfully before speaking again. "I think I need to borrow your letter from Evelyn one last time."

Will's body stiffened. "Caroline, I don't think that's a good idea."

"I don't have much time. I need to make a decision. Am I going to see the love of my life one more time before I die, or not?"

Will took a moment to think over what she'd just told him. So Caroline also had a long-lost love in the other timeline. As much as he identified with her struggle, he couldn't let her go to 1922 while he was supposed to be watching over her. "You know going there could hurt you. It could kill you! Lydia left me here to take care of you. I can't let you do this."

Caroline was silent for a few painfully long moments before she finally spoke again. "Don't you think Evelyn would do it for you?"

Chapter 29

1922

Evelyn woke up in the dead of night. It was dark, and she was still wearing her day clothes. As she sat on her bed rubbing her eyes, she groggily recalled her visit with Mariah. Her mother.

A pang of nausea overcame her when she recalled the woman she'd believed was her mother all her life was in fact a stranger who had been chosen to raise her. She had no idea how she'd ever approach the subject with the parents who had brought her up and given her everything. She understood why they'd kept her adoption a secret, but that didn't make it hurt less.

Evelyn wasn't sure what to do with herself. She didn't want to go back to bed. She'd just slept for hours. She was desperate to get everything off her chest. She checked the clock. It was one in the morning. Typically, Evelyn didn't miss the technological conveniences of 2003 much, but on nights like this, she would do anything to be able to open her laptop and search her list of friends to see who was awake and available to chat via instant message.

A lightbulb went on in her head. Her idea was potentially dangerous, but she was determined. And yearning to talk to someone who would understand. She picked up her gloves from the nightstand and slipped them on before carefully opening the closet door and pulling out Cecil's coat. Carrying it back to the bed with her, she stopped at the dresser and took the cork out of her jewelry box, sliding it into the pocket of the coat. Evelyn hoped whatever connection it had to the other timeline would help strengthen her ability to travel there without feeling so worn out afterward. She set an alarm to bring her back in thirty minutes. She wanted longer, but the warnings from Will and Caroline were still floating around in her mind.

Back on the bed, she took off her gloves and closed her eyes. She inhaled deeply, preparing for another flash forward. The moment Cecil's coat was wrapped around her shoulders, the bright light appeared, dazzling her. Within seconds, she was back in 2006.

The house was unfamiliar. She didn't recognize the furniture or the decor on the walls. Evelyn slowly scanned her surroundings to figure out where the flash had taken her. The only thing she knew for sure was that Will was nearby. Her ears perked up at voices speaking softly from somewhere in the house. She ventured down a hallway lined with art, getting closer to the voices as she went. Finally, she came to an open doorway. She carefully peeked in and cried out in happiness when she laid eyes on Will and Caroline, who both jumped at the sound.

"Evelyn!" Will ran to her and pulled her into a tight embrace. She hugged him back, closing her eyes and savoring the scent of his cologne. It was one of her favorite things, and she'd missed it so much. After a few blissful moments, they separated, and Evelyn approached Caroline's bedside. She leaned down and hugged the older woman. "Caroline, are you all right?"

"Oh, I'll be fine. My little visit to you the other night might have been too ambitious for this old body." She chuckled to herself.

"I feel responsible!" Evelyn said. "Is there anything I can do to help?"

"Never mind me. We've been discussing *you*. How are you holding up after the shock of your adoption information?"

"I talked to Mariah."

Will quickly came over to Evelyn and put his arm around her shoulders to comfort her. "How did it go?"

"She told me why they sent me away. Mariah caught Doctor Fle—my father—doing dreamer research and experiments on me behind her back. She said it was hurting me and she threatened to leave him and take me with her. Their compromise was to have me go and live with people who had nothing to do with the dreams and keep me far away from the research." She paused, her eyes downcast. "She was trying to protect me."

Caroline sighed. "Being a mother truly is the most difficult job in the entire world. Try to understand. She would have done anything to keep you safe."

Evelyn's voice was unsteady. "It just hurts."

Caroline sat up and took Evelyn's hand in her own. "I know. But you're strong. Stronger than most. You *are* going to be okay." Will slid his arm off her shoulder and took her other hand. Evelyn hadn't been supported like this in a long time. She squeezed both Will's and Caroline's hands, not wanting to let go.

The flash of white was brighter this time than it had ever been, and Evelyn cringed and squinted at the impact on her eyes. She didn't understand. It was too soon. It hadn't been thirty minutes. As though falling down a deep hole, her body became light as air, and she felt like she was spinning. When the light finally faded, she blinked a few times to get her bearings. She was back in her apartment in 1922.

It took her a few more seconds to realize she wasn't alone.

Chapter 30

1922

"What is this?" Thomas barked, his eyes darting from Evelyn to Caroline to Will. The three of them were still holding hands as they had been in Caroline's bedroom, only now they were in Evelyn's bedroom. In 1922. Thomas was wearing nothing but boxers and an undershirt. Evelyn had never seen him so exposed. The sight was slightly jarring after all this time with little physical intimacy. Coming back to reality, she quickly put together that Thomas must have come over while she was asleep, then come into her bedroom while she was in her flash forward and interrupted it, bringing her back here early. Along with two other people from 2006. It was a lot to take in, even for her, so she could imagine Thomas's confusion.

Evelyn let go of Will's and Caroline's hands and ran to Thomas, grabbing his arm. "Thomas, I didn't know this would happen! I have no idea how they got here!"

"Who are they?" He was breathing fast, and his fists were balled tightly. Evelyn let go of him.

She swallowed, nervous to introduce Thomas to Will. She'd always imagined them meeting and even wondered if they'd like one another, but she'd never thought it would actually happen. Especially not like this. Now that the moment had arrived, she was terrified. She bought herself a few seconds by introducing Caroline first. "Thomas, this is Caroline Huber." Thomas's eyes widened.

"From the dreamer studies?"

"Yes." Evelyn paused. She wasn't sure if he had another question. Thomas was silent.

"And this," she said as she finally gestured toward Will, "is Will Jenkins."

The color drained from Thomas's face, and Evelyn found herself struggling to say anything more. Thomas ran his hand over his mouth as he contemplated his response. After a few brutally silent moments, he turned on his heel and stormed out of the room.

Evelyn kicked Cecil's coat under her bed before she ran after Thomas, glancing back at Will and Caroline as she went. In the living room, Thomas had already pulled his pants on and was putting on his shoes.

"Thomas, don't go!"

He finished with his shoes and walked toward the front door to grab his coat. He said nothing.

"Just talk to me! Please!" Evelyn's voice trembled.

He stopped with his hand on the doorknob, not turning back to face her. "I'm listening."

"I had no one to talk to. It was the middle of the night and—"

"I was right here!" He whipped around to face her.

"How was I supposed to know that? I was fast asleep!"

"You weren't supposed to be visiting your other timeline at all, Evelyn!"

She couldn't argue. He was right. She had promised him she wouldn't flash forward on her own anymore. At least not until they knew more about the consequences. She stared at the buttons on his shirt, unable to bring herself to meet his eyes. "I know."

"What exactly do you want me to do right now?" He sounded defeated.

"Stay! Meet them. Talk to them." She put her hand softly on his chest. "So we can figure it out. So we can figure *us* out."

He sighed and breathed deeply into his hands. "I've never wanted to meet anyone less."

She removed her hand. "I know it's awkward. Impossible, even. I'll understand if you can't."

He looked up at the ceiling and groaned in exasperation. "I said I'd do whatever it took to be with you. I suppose this is what it's going to take."

She hugged him tightly. "Thank you. I'm sorry." She knew she was asking him to do something every shred of his being would want to run from, but it was happening, and with Will here, it was completely unavoidable.

Soon, the foursome was seated in Evelyn's living room, tension heavily clouding the proceedings. Evelyn was on the couch with Thomas to her right and Will to her left on a separate chair. She'd spent so much time back and forth between these two men in a figurative sense that it was surreal to be *literally* between them. She was afraid her heart would thump out of her chest. She tried to calm her nerves with a deep breath before she finally broke the silence.

"Where to begin?" She bit her lip. "I suppose I should start by apologizing to everyone. Thomas, I'm sorry to put you in this position. Will and Caroline, I'm sorry you've somehow been caught up in my flashes." For the first time, it dawned on her that this was all probably a major shock for Will. He had never visited another timeline. He'd never been to the 1920s. He'd barely spoken since they arrived, and she scolded herself for throwing him into this and not being more sensitive. "Will, I know this must all be a huge shock. Are you okay?"

"It's . . . a lot." He smiled weakly, his arms folded tightly across his chest.

"I'm going to figure out how to get you back home," Evelyn promised. She hoped she wasn't lying. The truth was she didn't know if she could do it. He wasn't a dreamer, and she still didn't have anymore answers from Holstead about her own powers to travel. Evelyn had no idea how the news that she could transport two humans at once would affect Holstead's findings.

Caroline interrupted. "Evelyn, might I suggest we leave the gentlemen alone to have a word?"

Evelyn glanced at Thomas to gauge his reaction. He did not appear ruffled at the idea of talking to Will one on one, and she hoped that was a good sign.

"Let's go into the kitchen." Caroline stood, and Evelyn followed suit. Evelyn caught Will's eye as she left the room, quietly reassuring him everything would be okay. Thomas's mood had been rather unpredictable lately, and this wasn't exactly an everyday circumstance.

In the kitchen with Caroline, Evelyn leaned on the counter and put her face in her hands. Her worlds had finally collided. She'd imagined it a million times but never thought Will could actually be here. The gravity of what she'd done by going to 2006 was weighing on her heavily. "What am I going to do?"

Caroline put her hand gently on Evelyn's shoulder. "Surely you have the power to get Will back home. You've always been able to do more than the other dreamers. That's why Doctor Fletcher was so intent on studying your abilities. You're not like the rest of us!"

Evelyn dropped her hands and looked up. "Until tonight I didn't know I could transport other people through time. How is that even possible?"

"I'm not sure. But if you can bring them here, you must be able to get them back, right? We just need to find out how!"

Evelyn nodded and eyed the doorway to the living room. "I hope they're okay in there."

In the living room, Thomas and Will's conversation was slow to start. Neither was exactly sure how to articulate the complicated and unusual circumstances in which they found themselves. Will took in the apartment and its 1920s furnishings. He was both nervous and fascinated.

Thomas made a show of moving decorative pillows around on the couch to make it more comfortable for himself, clearly stalling for time.

Eventually Will spoke up. "I'm really sorry to just show up here like this. I don't know how it happened, but this obviously wasn't planned."

Thomas cleared his throat and shifted in his seat. "I know. I apologize for my earlier reaction."

"Look, I understand things are weird between us. I know you probably hate me—"

"I don't hate you."

Will stared at him, unsure how to respond. Thomas continued. "I suppose I really should be thanking you."

"Thanking me?" It was the last thing he'd expected Thomas to say.

"For being there for Evelyn when she was losing her other life. For helping her through it on the other side." He took a breath. "For loving her when she needed it most."

"I would do it a thousand times over."

"I know. So would I. All of this. As balled up as this whole thing is, I think we both know she's worth it."

Will nodded. The two sat in strained silence for several excruciating seconds before Will finally spoke again. "I'm sorry if it ever got uncomfortable for you on this side."

Thomas scoffed. "It hasn't stopped being uncomfortable, has it?" They both chuckled. As much as it annoyed Thomas, he liked Will. He could see why Evelyn did, too.

"How is she?" Will asked.

"What do you mean?"

"Here. In this life. Is she okay after she lost everything in the other timeline?"

Thomas gazed down at the coffee table. "When it first happened, she was a shell of herself. I wasn't sure if she'd ever come out of it. I did everything I could to help, but in the end, it was time that did the most healing. It's much better now. Well, it was until the last couple of weeks. I'm worried that this news about the Fletchers will be the breaking point. The thing that sends her right back to the beginning so she has to claw her way out again. And I'm scared that traveling between timelines in these flashes is going to harm her." He rubbed his hands over his face. "I feel so out of control, and I can sense her slipping away." Thomas stopped and inhaled sharply. "Forgive me."

"No, I get it! I've been worried, too. That the flashes—Caroline calls them daydreams—will hurt her. And that I'll have to lose her all over again."

Thomas's head snapped up. "You know, it never really occurred to me that you might have to lose her twice. I'm still not sure how you did it once. I'm sorry."

Will nodded, silent. There were no words for what he'd been through when Evelyn died.

Thomas was the first one to speak again. "For Evelyn's sake, maybe while we're here together, two heads are better than one."

"What are you saying?"

Thomas leaned forward and rested his elbows on his knees as he explained. "When Evelyn was still having the dreams, you and I did a pretty good job of uncovering answers in our respective timelines. Together, we were able to learn a lot about the dreams and how they worked. Now that we're in the same time and place, we could join forces to figure out the flashes. Make sure Evelyn will be safe, no matter where she is or who she's with."

Will mulled it over. He was still trying to figure out what to do about being in an alternate timeline and hadn't really had a moment to contemplate much else. But he would do anything for Evelyn, and he wasn't going to pass up an opportunity to make sure everything turned out fine for her, whether he was part of that future or not. "I'm in. If I think of anything that can help keep her safe, you'll be the first to know."

Thomas snickered. "You know, I really *wanted* to hate you."

"Same." Will smiled weakly.

"I never thought I'd be sitting here having a friendly chat with my fiancée's other love."

The smile disappeared from Will's face. "Oh, I didn't realize you were engaged."

Thomas opened his mouth to clarify that the engagement was technically off at the moment. Just then, a loud crash echoed from the kitchen. Will and Thomas both sprung up and dashed toward the clatter. When they got there, Evelyn was standing with her hands over her mouth, staring down at the spilled tea tray and all its contents on the floor. She was ashen and her body was shaking.

"I don't know what happened!" Caroline had her arm around Evelyn's waist, steadying her.

"I think I'm just weak from the visit to the other timeline," Evelyn said breathily. "I'm sure I'll be fine. I just need to lie down."

Thomas and Will both moved toward her and stopped, awkwardly trying to decide whether to allow the other to take the lead. Will stepped aside and let Thomas grab Evelyn and walk with her to the bedroom, leaving Will and Caroline to clean up the mess on the kitchen floor.

As Thomas helped Evelyn into bed, Will entered the room with a glass of water. He placed it on the nightstand and turned to face her. "Get some rest. I'm sure you'll be back to yourself soon." On his way to the bedroom door, Will spotted something on the end of the bed. He picked it up and examined it. It was the cork. And it was burnt.

Chapter 31

1922

They'd all had a bite to eat and some time to come to terms with their strange situation. Will and Thomas were even bantering back and forth a bit, which surprised and pleased Evelyn, who had mostly recovered from her dizzy spell earlier. The meeting between the two men had gone better than she ever could have predicted. She had to talk to Will about how to get him back to his own timeline, probably sooner rather than later, but selfishly she wished she could keep both of them here with her forever somehow.

Caroline cleared her throat. "I have something to tell you all." Everyone stopped what they were doing and gave her their full attention. "I can't go back to 2006."

Evelyn shook her head furiously. "Caroline, you have to. Your daughter!"

"It's not a matter of whether I want to go back or not," Caroline said sadly. "I can't."

Thomas leaned forward in his seat. "What's stopping you from flashing back to your timeline?"

Will spoke up before Caroline could answer. "Is this about the cancer?"

Evelyn's stomach dropped, and she turned to Caroline, her mouth agape.

Caroline sighed. All eyes were on her. "It's made me too weak. I can feel it in my body. Coming here must have been the last trip I had in me. The energy to daydream is completely gone."

"No! There must be some way to get you home! You need to see Lydia!" Evelyn looked at Thomas and Will, imploring them with her eyes to say something that would help. She would hate to be the reason Caroline didn't get to say goodbye to her child.

"It's not possible. You see, I've passed away in both timelines now, so my existence must cease to be. Everywhere."

"You asked me to borrow the letter before," Will said to Caroline. "This is what you wanted, isn't it? To come here one last time. You knew you might not be able to go back."

"I hadn't thought it would happen exactly like this. I thought I'd choose when and come alone, but yes." Caroline was clearly fighting tears. "I wanted this timeline to be my last stop."

"Why?" Evelyn's eyes were wide with incredulity.

Caroline pursed her lips, considering her answer. She finally spoke. "I told you I knew what it was like to leave someone you love in another time."

"You came to see him." Evelyn understood completely.

"For the first and last time since we parted all those years ago," Caroline said wistfully. "I haven't shown myself to him since I left this life, but I've visited in my daydreams. I've seen him. Now, I just want one last conversation. It was our parting agreement that if I could find a way to speak to him one more time before one of us left this world for good, I would do it."

A deafening silence filled the room as Thomas, Will, and Evelyn all came to grips with the fact that Caroline was right, and now they needed to help her fulfill her final wish.

Thomas stood. "How do we find him?"

"He's here, in the city. He's lived in the same place for decades."

"Well then, it's settled. We'll go and see him first thing in the morning."

Caroline looked up at him and bit her bottom lip, shaking her head. "I'm afraid we don't have that much time."

Will's head whipped toward her. "Why? What's going to happen?"

A sad smile came across Caroline's face. "I'm dead. My body can't be in two places at once." She paused to see if everyone would catch on, but no one spoke. "Dying in my other life means both my existences are gone now. There's nothing left of me, is there?"

Evelyn gasped. "You mean . . .?"

"I'm sure I only have a couple of hours here at most before I simply . . . vanish. Forever."

Will stood up as well, joining Thomas. "Then let's go!" Evelyn quietly steadied her breath and willed herself not to cry as she joined them and headed for the door.

It was dark and cold on the city streets. New York was different at night. The roads were empty and quiet, devoid of their usual lines of motor traffic, the sidewalks bare of their typical throngs of pedestrians. Evelyn had never been out this late at night alone and only a handful of times with other people. She much preferred the city in the daytime.

The four walked several blocks to the address Caroline knew by heart. Evelyn had given her a long coat to cover up her clothing from 2006 for the walk so she would blend in if anyone saw them. Will was wearing Thomas's long jacket.

The two men were walking a bit ahead of the women, engaged in talk about how different the city was in 2006. Evelyn's mind swirled with a million things she wanted to say to Caroline, but nothing seemed quite right, so she asked about the mystery man they were headed to see. "What's his name? How did you two meet?"

Caroline's eyes sparkled as she recalled the day. "His name is Benjamin. I met him at the opening of the inaugural line of the subway in 1904. I fell in love with him the moment I saw him from across the street."

"What happened?"

Caroline took a long pause before answering. "Our story is much like your story with Will."

Evelyn had no response. They shared an unspoken understanding of everything that meant.

As they approached the front door, Caroline turned to Evelyn. "Do I look all right?" Her voice shook slightly.

Evelyn carefully adjusted Caroline's hair and smiled sadly. "You look perfect."

"I suppose this is it."

They all stared at Caroline, unsure of what to say. The moment was as heartbreaking as it was beautiful, and words came up short. Will moved forward and hugged her. Thomas and Evelyn followed suit, the women both crying softly. Caroline took Evelyn's face in her hands as they parted and whispered, "You listen to your heart, do you hear me? You're stronger than you know. Choose *happiness*. Whatever that looks like for you."

Evelyn hugged the older woman one last time. "Thank you. For everything." Caroline was the only other dreamer Evelyn had ever met in person, and they shared a bond no one but another dreamer could ever understand.

They let go of each other, and Caroline turned to face the door of the house where her long-lost love, Benjamin, was sleeping. Thomas, Evelyn, and Will started their walk back the way they'd come, leaving Caroline to carry out her dying act. It had started raining very softly, a light mist covering the street. Evelyn stopped before they turned the corner and looked back down the block. She grabbed Thomas's arm. "Look!" she said, her lips parting slightly as her emotions lodged themselves painfully in her throat. Will and Thomas turned to see what she was pointing at.

In the dim light of a streetlamp, they watched as Benjamin stepped out of his house, confused. It was a bit far to see much, but from their vantage point, Evelyn clearly saw him take just one look at Caroline and the two collapsed into each other's arms. They held each other for what seemed like forever. Evelyn wiped the moisture from her eyes. She couldn't ignore the glaring parallels between Caroline and Benjamin's beautiful love story and the one she was still writing with Will. Their ending would probably be the same. Her mind was reeling as she processed everything she'd just witnessed, and it threatened to overwhelm her. She bit her lip hard to stop herself from letting go and sobbing in the middle of the damp city street. Instead she turned to leave. "We should go."

Chapter 32

1922

Evelyn was back in her apartment with Thomas and Will after they'd left Caroline with Benjamin. It was almost two o'clock in the morning and they were all exhausted. It was a strange experience, dropping someone off to die in another person's arms. Everything in her was telling Evelyn they'd done the right thing, both for Caroline and Benjamin.

Evelyn had no idea how she would navigate the sleeping situation with Thomas and Will both in her apartment. Thankfully, Thomas interjected.

"I think it's time to get to bed. I'm happy to host Will at my house in the guest room. We can all reconvene in the morning and figure out how to get him back home."

Evelyn raised her eyebrows at him. "And how do you propose we explain the time-traveling stranger from the future to your mother?"

Thomas bit the inside of his cheek. "I hadn't thought of that."

Evelyn answered for him. "No one else can know about this. We all need to go and see Doctor Holstead in the morning. I live closer to his house. Will can stay here." Thomas gave her a piercing glare. "On the sofa," Evelyn added quickly.

Will, fully aware of the tension, assured Thomas, "You've got nothing to worry about. You two are engaged. I'm out of it." He raised his hands in mock defeat. Evelyn gulped. She didn't know Will had found out about the engagement. She desperately wanted to explain it was currently off, but not in front of Thomas.

Thomas nodded, begrudgingly accepting Will's promise that nothing untoward would happen while he was gone. He took Evelyn's hand in his. "I'll see you in a few hours."

"Are you sure? You could stay, too," she implored, not wanting to upset him.

He glanced at Will, then turned to Evelyn. "You know it's not proper for me to stay without telling Edward why. He saw me come in, and so did some of your neighbors. They'd talk. We're lucky no one has seen us sneaking Will up and down the stairwell yet."

Evelyn shrugged. "I suppose you're right." She wondered if she should put up more of a fight for him to stay if for no other reason than to make him feel better, but she decided to leave it for now.

Thomas bid Will goodnight and kissed Evelyn's cheek before he left. "Everything in me is telling me not to leave him here with you."

She rubbed his upper arm. "It's going to be fine. I promise." They agreed he would return at eight o'clock the next morning to go to Holstead's.

The door clicked shut, leaving Evelyn and Will alone. She walked slowly into the living room, where he was still standing, his eyes intently on her. She stood across the coffee table from him, wringing her hands.

"You're engaged." He was smiling, trying to be congratulatory. His tone, however, conveyed a heavy sadness.

She couldn't clear things up quickly enough. "I—"

"You don't owe me an explanation. You're happy here in this life. That's what I wanted for you. Honestly, before you showed up in my apartment that day, I always thought you'd be married by now."

Her heart dropped. Not just because her long engagement was a sore spot, but also because it pained her to picture Will in 2006, sad and alone, thinking about her being happily married. "I was going to tell you about the engagement. I just hadn't had the chance. And I'm actually not technically engaged at the moment. We—"

"Evelyn, stop." He was moving toward her. When he was an arm's length away, he put his hand on her shoulder. "It's fine."

Irritated that he was touching her in such a platonic way, she shook him off. "It's not fine!" She turned away and covered her eyes with her hands so she could think more clearly. She finally removed them and faced him again. He was so close she could see his jaw clenching. "I'm still so in love with you it hurts." Her voice was barely audible.

"Don't—" Before he could finish his sentence, her lips were on his. In spite of their promises to Thomas, Evelyn was helpless to resist. Will kissed her back with all the passion he'd been bottling up for the last three years.

They eventually managed to pull away, breathing heavily, both their pulses racing.

She bit her lips, almost as if to hide them away from him so they couldn't meet his again. Eventually she found words. "I'm sorry. I shouldn't have done that."

He sat on the sofa and ran his hands through his hair. Finally, he leaned back and looked at her. "Can I just hold you?"

Her heart fluttered. She'd sorely missed spending the night in his arms. The idea that she could do it even one more time was a prize she coveted. She joined him, nestling into a warm snuggle the likes of which she had never enjoyed with Thomas. She'd missed this type of loving physical intimacy. It wasn't in Thomas's nature. He had his own brand of loving her. She tucked the nagging guilt away and allowed herself to lean into the moment. It was everything she'd secretly been imagining for years, and she simply couldn't let it pass her by.

Will gazed at the woman he loved more than anything in the world, the early dawn casting a romantic glow over her face through the bedroom curtains as she slept. After they'd kissed, they'd retired to her bed, where they talked for what seemed like hours. And then she'd finally drifted off in his arms, the way she had so many nights in their other timeline, and it was even more perfect than he remembered. He hadn't been able to sleep a wink.

In spite of his elation, thoughts of Thomas and his blind trust in Evelyn haunted Will as he lay with her. It had taken them less than ten minutes for them to break their word to him. He dreaded the fallout when Evelyn woke up. He knew her so well. She'd be ridden with remorse and sick with worry over what they'd done, and they'd have to hide it because Thomas was coming over and Will likely had to go back to 2006. Not that he was in any rush. He wished he'd exercised more self-control with Evelyn, but his emotions—and his hormones—had taken over when she kissed him, and he'd given in. He didn't necessarily regret it, but he was concerned that it might make Evelyn's life more complicated, and he'd never wanted to do that.

He took in her beauty. She appeared so at peace as she slept, but in her waking life she was in a constant state of emotional turmoil. He hated that for her. He also hated that he may have to say goodbye to her again soon. He used the opportunity to study everything about her so he would always remember. He'd missed even the little things about her. The gentle movement of her chest as she breathed. The way her lips parted slightly when she slept. Without thinking, he reached out and tenderly stroked her hair. She stirred and her eyes fluttered open. When she saw him, she smiled sleepily and nuzzled in closer. Evelyn fell back asleep. He finally closed his eyes, content that unlike last time they'd spent a night together, sleep wouldn't take her decades away from him.

Chapter 33

1922

Evelyn and Will had fifteen minutes before Thomas was due. She'd been strangely quiet since they'd woken up in each other's arms. They'd only kissed once the previous night and hadn't taken things further than sleeping in the same bed, but it was enough to send her into a spiral of guilt.

She emerged from her bedroom, dressed and ready to go to Holstead's. Will looked like he was still freshly out of 2006, which would obviously catch attention as they walked to Holstead's house. Thomas was supposed to bring over a change of clothes for him to avoid any trouble. She smoothed her skirt as she walked over to sit on the couch next to him. "Is it strange for you, seeing me dressed this way?"

He laughed softly. "A little."

"I miss my clothes from the other life." She shifted in her seat, fidgeting with her engagement ring out of habit.

"Let's talk about what's really on your mind." Will knew her too well. She couldn't hide anything from him.

She folded her arms tightly across her chest. "I don't want you to go back."

He stared into her eyes. "I don't want to go back."

"What if you didn't have to? Would you stay?"

He licked his lips and considered it for a moment before he answered. "I would do *anything* to be with you again."

They sat in silence for a few seconds. They weren't touching. Eventually Evelyn spoke up. "I have to tell Thomas about last night."

His eyes widened. "No, come on. Don't blow up your whole life because of one kiss, or because of me. I'll probably be gone soon. Please. You need to be happy. Here. Now."

"He deserves to know. And I'm not sure I *am* happy here."

"What are you talking about?"

"Thomas and me. We've been . . . growing apart. He's opening his practice, and he works so much. I'm doing everything by myself, and I miss working at the law office! It's just—" She sighed. "It's just not the same as it was with you."

"Evelyn, you can't compare it."

"It's not the same, Will!" She hadn't meant to raise her voice. "I'm sorry. I just can't lie to you." She shook her head. "There's always been something missing between me and Thomas. Even before I lost the other life."

He struggled for the right words. "You don't have to marry him if you're not happy. You can back out. But please, don't let it be because of me. If you choose not to be with him, it should be because he's not the one for you."

"He's right for me in so many ways." She ran her fingertips over the diamond on her engagement ring. "I do love him."

"I know."

"He loves me."

"I can see that."

"I don't want to hurt him. I'm terrified that I'm going to, one way or another."

A knock on the door interrupted their talk. Evelyn hesitated before she got up to answer it. She cupped Will's face in her hand, admiring him and taking one last moment with him alone before she had to give him up to 2006. Or, she hoped, not. After a few seconds, she turned and walked to the door.

Thomas came in carrying a duffel bag containing the change of clothes he'd brought for Will. He greeted Evelyn with a peck on the cheek and sent Will a brief smile and handed the bag over. "I hope it all fits."

"Thanks. I appreciate it," Will said, taking it. "I'll go change." He retreated to the bedroom and closed the door, leaving Thomas and Evelyn alone in a stiff silence.

She sat back on the sofa. Thomas walked to the window and stared out of it, not saying a word. Evelyn couldn't take it anymore. "How did you sleep?"

He kept looking out of the window. "Not well."

"I'm sorry this is happening." She'd already apologized the night before, but she couldn't think of a single other thing to say.

He turned to her and smiled, but not the warm, inviting smile she was used to. It was forced and a little resentful. "I suppose this is what I signed up for, isn't it?"

She could read the anger in Thomas's words, and it broke her that she'd acted so selfishly, kissing Will. Staring at her hands, she wished she could erase all the heartache she'd ever caused Thomas. "Thank you for staying by my side. I know it's not easy."

He didn't answer. A few moments later, the bedroom door clicked open and Will emerged, clad in a collared shirt and tie with a three-piece suit, holding a golf cap in his hands. Evelyn's body tingled at how handsome he was. She'd never imagined how he might look in the clothes from this era, and she was pleasantly surprised.

"We'd better get going," Thomas said, already headed for the door. It was clear to both Will and Evelyn that he was eager to get Will back to his own timeline and get the ordeal over with. They followed him, locking the apartment door behind them.

Out on the city streets for the first time in daylight, Will was mesmerized by the sights of 1922 New York. He was seeing the past in real time. The city he was used to was unimaginably different. The cars, the buildings, and even the smells were worlds apart from his New York, and he marveled aloud at how much industrialization and technology would advance in the next several decades. Will's wide eyes and the way he stared at everything they passed gave him away as a visitor to the city. As he walked with Evelyn and Thomas to Holstead's house, and in spite of his attempts, he also couldn't hide from Evelyn the fact that he was extremely anxious. She understood why. It was the same reason for her own nervousness. If Holstead told them there was a way to go back to 2006, Thomas would surely make a push for him to go as soon as possible. She tried her best not to think about it and told herself to let things play out.

The trio made small talk on the way. Evelyn was careful to avoid discussing what happened after Thomas left her apartment the night before and was glad to stop steering the conversation when they finally arrived at Doctor Holstead's front door.

Mrs. Brooks was surprised but delighted to see Thomas and Evelyn. They introduced Will as a friend, and, to their relief, she didn't ask any questions about him.

She ushered them inside. "Have you three had breakfast?"

Evelyn smiled. Mrs. Brooks was a perpetual mother hen, always making sure everyone was taken care of. "Not yet. We got a bit of an early start today."

"Well, I'll whip you up something while you wait for the doctor!" She opened the door to the sitting room and gestured for them to go inside. "I'll go tell him you're here."

The three sat. Thomas was sure to place himself next to Evelyn, forcing Will to sit across from them.

With every second that passed, Evelyn became more emotional at the idea of Will having to go back. Having him here, in her real life and not just in her memories or her daydreams, was exactly what she'd longed for since the moment she'd left him in 2003. She could see him. Touch him. And when she'd kissed him a few hours before, it had sparked something inside her she hadn't felt in years. And she relished the way that feeling washed over her and made everything better. Letting him go—again—was the last thing she wanted to do.

Before the three had a chance to strike up a conversation, Doctor Holstead entered the room.

"Good morning!" He paused when he saw Will. "Ah, who do we have here?"

Will stood up and held out his hand. "I'm Will. Will Jenkins."

Holstead's eyes grew wide as he registered the name and its implications. He turned to Evelyn, waiting for her to explain how Will could possibly be here.

"I didn't mean to!" she said quickly. "I got interrupted while I was in a flash, and he came back with me!"

Holstead took a moment to consider her story. "You actually . . . transported a non-dreamer . . . across timelines?" She nodded. He took a moment, mulling over the magnitude of the development. "Incredible!" he cried.

Thomas scoffed. "It is astounding, but it's also time to get Will back to where he belongs."

The tinge of rudeness annoyed Evelyn. She understood Thomas was in a difficult spot, and he'd been patient so far, but the least he could do was try not to make Will uncomfortable. After all, it wasn't his fault he was in this timeline. Then she remembered she'd kissed Will the night before and quietly gave Thomas a bit more grace.

Thomas clarified. "Doctor Holstead, can you help us figure out if there's any way for Will to get back to 2006?"

Holstead adjusted his glasses. "I suppose the obvious answer is that you get him back home the same way he got here."

Evelyn nodded. "I thought so, too. I just wasn't sure if it would be too dangerous. For me or for Will."

Before Holstead could respond, Will fished something out of his pocket and presented it to the group. The charred cork lay on his palm, black and damaged from its journeys back and forth through time with Evelyn. "I don't want to end up like this."

Seeing the cork in its damaged state for the first time filled Evelyn with an avalanche of emotions. Fear that she and Will would get hurt trying to get him home, surprise that Will hadn't shared the changed cork with her before now, and sadness that one of her most treasured keepsakes from her relationship with him was ruined.

Holstead ran his hand over his beard as he contemplated the predicament. "Let's go to my office."

Chapter 34

1922

Evelyn sat in one of the two chairs across Holstead's desk as the doctor leafed hurriedly through the papers they'd pulled from Fletcher's office. Thomas and Will both stood, neither moving to take the remaining seat. They'd explained to him everything that happened the night before. He had asked a long string of questions and though he tried, Holstead had been unable to hide his astonishment at each new development in the story.

"Doctor, what do you think will happen to Will if he stays here too long?" Evelyn asked as Holstead flipped through the research. He stopped to ponder her question.

"I don't know, but based on the state of the cork, I can't imagine traveling again would do much good for either of you." He patted the stack of files in front of him. "I want to count how many flashes each dreamer had before they . . . stopped. It might give us some indication of how many trips back and forth across timelines dreamers can withstand before it becomes too much." He looked up from the papers. "Did anyone ask Caroline how many times she traveled back to this timeline after she lost her dreams?"

"I spoke to her about it a bit," Will answered. "She didn't give me a number, but it sounded like she tried to go as little as possible. I think the flashes scared her. She didn't like the energy drain afterward. I think she was also scared of losing the ability to see Benjamin one last time."

Holstead nodded. "If Caroline only visited a handful of times, I can't imagine Evelyn has much more traveling ahead. Evelyn is, according to everything we know now, a more powerful dreamer than most, so it's possible she could withstand a few more trips than Caroline or another dreamer, but every trip would be a big risk. And that's not even considering the fact that Evelyn would also be transporting Will with her, which would further drain her energy."

Evelyn glanced from Holstead to Thomas to Will. "Isn't it dangerous for Will, too?" she asked.

Holstead shrugged and shook his head. "We have no way of knowing how traveling across timelines affects a non-dreamer. Regardless, I can't imagine the cork bodes well for Will's physical wellbeing, if I'm being frank."

Evelyn clenched her jaw and looked over at Will to gauge how he was handling all the news. Holstead was all but telling them that taking Will home was possibly perilous for them both. Even more guilt was building up inside her over accidentally bringing him here and putting him in this inconceivable situation.

Holstead returned his attention to the research on his desk. "The only part of this I haven't gone through yet is these last few dozen pages. If there's no answer here about a safer way to get Will home, I'm not sure there *is* another answer." He pulled out the last few pages and sat back in his chair, adjusting his spectacles again so he could read through them. The quiet in the room was tense and painstaking while they all waited for Holstead to reveal whether he'd found anything. Finally, he replaced the papers on his desk and returned to his seat. "There might be one way."

Holstead explained that Will could get back to 2006 using a combination of the way Evelyn first flashed to his timeline and the way she'd accidentally brought him to this one. "Evelyn would need to be physically in contact with you at the same time she came into contact with an object that prompted the flashes. The object can't be just anything. It must be something of significance to you, Will. I'm not sure how easy it will be to find something like that here. Unless of course you reveal yourself."

Evelyn furrowed her brow. "You mean talk to Cecil?"

"Well, that would be the only obvious answer, in my estimation."

"I don't know." Will was starting to panic. "Every time-travel movie says not to do things that could change the future. Wouldn't meeting my actual ancestor be pushing those boundaries a little too far?"

"I haven't seen any time-travel films myself," Holstead replied. "But I agree revealing yourself to Cecil is risky in its own ways."

Evelyn stared down at the research on the desk, her mind on overdrive as she considered the ramifications of introducing Will to Cecil. How would she possibly explain it? Then it hit her. "The coat!"

"Coat?" Holstead and Thomas asked in unison.

Evelyn hadn't revealed to Holstead and Thomas yet that she'd stolen Cecil's coat from the bank. She wasn't exactly proud of it. "I think I have something that could get Will back to his timeline."

Thomas, Evelyn, and Will said their goodbyes to Holstead and took a brisk walk back to her apartment. As usual, they took the stairs to avoid Edward and other residents. Once inside, Evelyn put on her gloves and made a beeline for her bedroom to retrieve Cecil's coat from under the bed, where she'd kicked it after her surprise return from 2006. When she came into the living room, Thomas and Will were sitting separately. Thomas was leaning forward with his hands clasped and his elbows on his knees, eager to get the whole ordeal over with. Will was leaning back on the sofa with his arms folded, staring straight ahead. They hadn't spoken since Evelyn left the room.

"Here it is," she said, holding up the coat. "Holstead said all we have to do is touch when I wear this, and we should go back to your timeline." She couldn't mask the hint of sadness in her voice when she said it.

Thomas cleared his throat. "How long should I wait until I get you back here?" His role in the plan was to make sure Evelyn returned without spending too long in 2006, so she wouldn't be unwell when she got back, like last time. He at least hoped to minimize the effects of her traveling across timelines.

"No more than half an hour," Evelyn replied, still holding the coat. "That should give us enough time to make sure it's worked and that Will is okay." She was struggling to keep her voice steady, but her time with Will was ticking away, and she couldn't think of a single thing to say to Thomas that would make him change his mind about wanting Will to go home.

Will chimed in. "And to make sure you're all right."

Evelyn smiled. "Yes. That, too." It was typical of him to be thinking of her instead of himself.

Thomas stood. "Should we get this over with?" Evelyn's cheeks flushed, embarrassed at how brash Thomas was being. Noting her expression, Thomas added, "Will has already been here for hours. We don't know what that will do to him."

"He's right," Will said. He stood and joined Evelyn. "We should go."

She swallowed and gathered herself. As much as Evelyn didn't want to part with Will, Thomas's discomfort was growing by the second, and they were all exceedingly aware of it.

After they all got into their respective positions, Will paused. "So, when we're gone, what does that look like for you on this side?"

Thomas shrugged. "You and Evelyn are different. She's a dreamer, so her body can be in two places at once. She stays here *and* goes there. It just looks like she's asleep. You can only be in one timeline, so you probably just . . . disappear."

Will raised his eyebrows. "Wow." He looked from Evelyn to Thomas and back at her. "I guess it's time."

"Yes, I suppose so." Her entire frame drooped as she spoke.

To her surprise, Thomas extended his hand to Will. "It was good to finally put a face to the name."

Will shook his hand firmly. "Likewise." The two shared a look that Evelyn imagined only two men who loved the same woman could mutually understand. "Take care of her."

Thomas nodded. "Always."

They released their handshake and Will turned to Evelyn, ready for his journey back to 2006. "Shall we do this?"

"I suppose so." She handed Will the coat, removed her gloves and carefully placed them on the chair in front of her. She needed her skin to be touching Will for this to work. She reached for his hand, glancing at Thomas as she did. Thomas looked away. Evelyn sighed and turned to Will. "Ready?"

They sat on the sofa together. He gripped her hand tighter, and she looked at Thomas again. "Okay, now." Thomas picked up the coat and wrapped it around her shoulders.

Immediately Will and Evelyn were both engulfed in the blinding light. Will moaned as the energy surged through them both. Within seconds, the light disappeared, and they found themselves in his apartment. They stood, hand in hand, scanning their surroundings to make sure they had arrived in the right place and time.

"It worked!" Evelyn said.

"Yeah, it really did!" He squeezed her hand and let go, slowly walking around the room, examining it to confirm. "So now what?"

She shrugged. "I'm not sure. We have thirty minutes before Thomas brings me back. I suppose the safest thing to do is just . . . wait here."

He came back to where she was standing and gently pulled her arm, motioning for her to join him on the couch. "Will you ever be able to come back?"

She began to speak but wasn't sure what to say. "I know I should say no. For Thomas. And for you. It's not fair to either of you to keep visiting this timeline. But I also know how hard it is for me to resist flashing forward to see you knowing the possibility exists, even if it harms me."

"Holstead said you'll deteriorate if you travel between the timelines too much," Will reminded her. "I don't want to be the reason you get hurt."

Evelyn shifted to sit closer, facing him. "How can I live there, pretending to be happy, all the while knowing you're here?"

"Thomas is a good man, Evelyn. You deserve that. I told you before, I won't be the reason you throw away your entire life there."

Evelyn's eyes were ablaze with a thousand things she wanted to say to him, but no words could ever be enough. So she kissed him.

Chapter 35

2006

Evelyn was lost in the moment with Will. Being so far away from her 1922 life was freeing and empowering. With his mouth on hers, she completely ignored the pangs of conscience tugging at her from the other timeline.

A loud knock on Will's apartment door startled them out of each other's arms.

"NYPD! Open up!"

They glanced at each other, concerned and confused. Will put his hands on her shoulders and shuffled her toward the bathroom door. "Hide. You're not supposed to be alive in this timeline, remember?"

She nodded, the hairs on her neck standing up, and hid in his bathroom. With the door cracked only a few millimeters, she peered through and kept an eye on Will.

He threw off his jacket and suspenders so he looked less suspicious in the clothing from the 1920s. He checked the peephole before opening the door. Two uniformed police officers were standing outside. One was tall and built, the other shorter and stockier. Will didn't step aside to let them in. "Good evening, Officers. What can I do for you?"

"William Jenkins?" asked the taller officer, eyeing Will's strange garb.

"Yes."

"I'm Officer Lopez, and this is Officer Thorpe. We have some questions to ask you about the death of Caroline Huber."

Evelyn's blood ran cold as she watched from her hiding spot. Will raced to come up with a response. "Caroline? She's dead?" Evelyn closed her eyes in silent thanks that he'd chosen to play dumb.

Thorpe nodded. "Died yesterday. At her home in Saugerties. It appeared to be of natural causes, but her daughter seems to think otherwise."

Will raised his eyebrows. "Lydia? Wait, she thinks I had something to do with it?"

"According to her, you were the last person to see her mother alive. She believes Mrs. Huber was fine before she went out and left Caroline in your care."

"Caroline was sick, but she was alive when I left!" He ran his hands through his hair. He always did that when he was nervous.

"Why would you leave her alone if her daughter left her in your care?" Thorpe asked.

Will fumbled for a cover story. "Lydia was only supposed to be gone a few minutes, but it had been a long time. I had to get back to the city," he lied. "I had some work to catch up on."

The officers briefly glimpsed at one another. "And where do you work?" Lopez appeared unconvinced.

"I'm a policy analyst at the United Nations."

"Doesn't sound like a job that requires much nighttime work."

"Time zones. Making policy with people across the globe can get tricky."

The officers nodded. Thorpe spoke up for the first time. "Look, off the record, we think the daughter is grasping at straws, trying to pin her mom's death on someone. She can't accept it. It happens. But we still have to follow up. I'm sure you understand."

"Do I need to get a lawyer?" Will was clearly hesitant to say anything more without legal representation in spite of the officers' nonchalance.

"Up to you. We might have to come back and ask you some questions before this investigation wraps up. Don't leave the city in the next few days," Lopez said.

"I have nothing more to tell you, but I'm happy to answer any questions you think of. With my attorney present, of course."

"Of course. Have a good night, Mr. Jenkins." Lopez nodded at Will, and the officers walked down the hall toward the elevator. Inside, Will leaned his back against the door and exhaled in relief and also disbelief. He made his way to the bathroom door to tell Evelyn they were gone, but she was already on her way to him.

"Is Lydia serious? How could she accuse you of that?"

"I never even considered she would think I did it!" Will waved his arms in exasperation. "I wasn't there when Lydia found the body! I was with you, in 1922, but I *was* the last one to see Caroline alive in this timeline. I guess Lydia thinks because I was gone when she got back that I had something to do with Caroline dying!"

Evelyn bit her lip, contemplating their dilemma. "What should we do?"

"I don't know. I'll handle it. Right now, we have to make sure you get back to 1922 before anyone sees you and before being here too long starts to hurt you."

Her eyes lowered. Thomas was going to bring her back from this timeline soon regardless, but she wasn't ready to leave Will, and he wasn't ready for her to go. He cupped her chin gently with his fingers and raised her eyes up to him. "I don't want it to end, either."

"How much longer do we have?"

He checked his phone. "About fifteen minutes."

Evelyn's stomach dropped. That wasn't enough time. It would never be enough.

He headed for the dresser and pulled out some jeans and a T-shirt. "I'd better change in case the police come back. It won't be so easy to explain away these clothes if they ask."

As he undressed, she took in every inch of his body with her eyes. She missed him in so many ways, and in that moment, the physical was high on her list. Aside from the way Will's nearness always made her more whole, the social constraints of her other timeline had kept her from exploring her relationship with Thomas in a physical sense. It was something she'd shared with Will that Thomas couldn't possibly give her until they were married. At least not without the risk of being fodder for city gossip and putting his new practice at risk. She'd been missing the intimate connection she shared with Will and had years of pent-up energy waiting to be released. Her breath became shallower with every move he made as he changed his clothes, his skin beckoning her to touch it. She swallowed, her mouth suddenly dry.

He tugged on his jeans, still shirtless, and caught her staring at him. Shirt in hand, he crossed the room and stood in front of her. "I've missed you, too."

Unable to resist the closeness of his bare torso to her, she raised her hands and ran them softly and slowly over his chest. She remembered every familiar curve and crevice. Every freckle she'd been dreaming of since she'd lost him.

Before she could act on any of her desires, they were interrupted by yet another knock at the door. Will exhaled sharply, annoyed. "They're back already? What do they want?" Evelyn hid back in the bathroom. Will pulled the T-shirt over his head and barely had it all the way on as he opened the door. "Officers, I already tol—"

He was cut off as Lydia barged in past him, shoving him aside. Before he could say anything, she reached behind her and revealed a handgun. Evelyn had to clap her hand over her own mouth to stop from screaming out loud. Her heart was thudding in her chest as she peered through the tiny crack in the bathroom door. Lydia's hand was shaking as she pointed the gun toward Will. He instinctively put his hands in the air to show her he was no threat. "Lydia, I swear I didn't do anything to your mother. You have to believe me."

"Shut up!" Lydia barked, the whites of her eyes large and bloodshot. "You and those *stupid* dreams! As soon as I saw those useless cops leave here without you in handcuffs, I knew they weren't going to help me. So tell me the truth! What happened to my mother?" She was still aiming the gun at Will, who had backed himself up against the closed apartment door.

Evelyn's heart was now beating so hard her breath was shaky. She couldn't bear being so useless in this situation. She racked her brain as she peered through the crack in the door to figure out how she could help Will without anyone getting hurt.

Lydia's voice boomed again. "What happened to my mother?!"

"I—I don't know," Will stuttered. "She was fine when I left."

"Liar!" Her shout scared Evelyn, who jumped and almost knocked the bathroom door shut. She froze to make sure Lydia hadn't heard anything. All Evelyn wanted in the world was to see that Will didn't come to any harm.

Will lowered his arms, his back still pressed against the door. He looked Lydia in the eyes. "Your mom told me she had cancer. Her doctor just told her. I didn't do anything."

Lydia blinked. "I don't believe you. Why would she tell *you* that?"

"You didn't know?" Will saw an opportunity to disarm her, if not physically, then emotionally. "She probably didn't want to worry you. Caroline loved you so much. She told me so many times."

Lydia stared at him, the gun still inches from his chest. Evelyn held her breath as she waited for Lydia to respond. It was a few seconds that felt more like hours before Lydia finally made her decision about whether she believed Will or not. "No. No! You're lying!"

Evelyn's legs were limp for a moment as Lydia pushed the barrel of the gun against Will's torso.

Will flinched. "She said the cancer was in her pancreas and it was spreading fast. I swear on my life!"

Lydia squeezed her eyes shut as if to block out what he was saying. When she opened them again, she shifted her arm and pointed the gun at the couch. "Sit."

His arms back up, he walked carefully to the couch and sat down, never taking his eyes off Lydia. She sat in the armchair diagonally across from him, leaning on the armrest, still holding the gun. Evelyn could see she was on the verge of tears.

"I'm sorry you lost her," Will said quietly. "I know you're hurting."

"You have no idea how I feel!" Lydia's nostrils flared. "You don't know what it's like to have the dreams ruin your entire life!" Will said nothing, and Evelyn hoped Lydia would keep talking. If she kept speaking, she probably wouldn't shoot. Lydia took a deep breath and continued. "The dreams made my father leave. They made my mother sick. And now they've killed her, and I have nothing left. The dreams have taken *everything* from me!"

"I understand that more than you know."

Lydia scoffed. "How?"

"I lost the love of my life to the dreams, remember? That's why I came to talk to your mother in the first place. I miss Evelyn every day. So much it hurts. The dreams have taken everything from me, too." He paused. Lydia hadn't moved and her eyes were trained on him. He carried on. "I'm sorry. I know you hate the dreams. But you have to believe me. It was just a coincidence that your mother died the same night I visited." It was all Evelyn could do not to burst out of the bathroom and tell Lydia the truth about her mother. That she'd died exactly the way she'd wanted. In the arms of her true love, eighty-four years in the past. Will was still talking. "I wish things could have been different for you. You didn't deserve to have your life upended by the dreams. None of us do."

A wave of sadness hit Evelyn as she listened from the bathroom. She hoped Will was just trying to placate Lydia. If this was how he really felt about the dreams, she would never be able to forgive herself for wrapping him up in all of it. She tried to steady her shaky breathing as she waited for Lydia's response.

Lydia squeezed her eyes shut and processed Will's words before looking at him again. "If you knew the dreams caused so much heartbreak, why would you bring them back into my mother's life? Into mine?" She was starting to get loud again. "Why would you hurt more people with those ridiculous dreams?!" She stood up from the armchair, the gun still pointed at Will. "She was fine until you showed up at our door!" Tears were running down her face, which was red with fury. Her fingers were so tight around the gun her knuckles had turned white.

Will was breathing fast and starting to panic. "Lydia, please. Don't do anything you're going to regret."

"I regret ever opening my front door to *you*!" She raised the gun once more and put her finger on the trigger, ready to put an end to Will and the dreams once and for all. Before she could pull it, her body jerked forward from a strong impact from behind, causing the gun to fly from her hand, clattering to the floor.

Evelyn was on top of Lydia, trying to hold her down. "Will! Get the gun!"

He was already diving for the weapon. Lydia outweighed Evelyn and easily overtook her, pinning Evelyn to the floor. She got up and scrambled to retrieve the gun before Will could get to it, but she was a second too late. He towered over Lydia, weapon in hand. He didn't point it at her but held it up over his head with his fingers open to show he didn't intend to fire it. "Lydia, it's over. Go home and we'll forget the whole thing, okay?"

She glared up at him from the floor. "You expect me to forget that you killed my mom?" she snarled. "I won't forget. Ever. I'll hunt you down until the day I die if that's what it takes. You and every dreamer I can find!" Her jaw was tight, and she was breathing hard.

Evelyn stood and joined Will. "Killing the dreamers won't bring your mother back. The dreams have taken just as much from us as they have from you."

"Who the hell are *you*?"

"It doesn't matter. Just know that your mother was one of the kindest, most selfless people I ever met. She wouldn't want this for you." Evelyn was holding out hope that they could get Lydia out of Will's apartment before she hurt someone. Or herself.

Lydia stood up, slowly. Will lowered the hand that was holding the gun. He carefully and deliberately placed it down on the end table next to him, nodding at Lydia as a show of good faith. "She's right. Caroline wouldn't want you to spend the rest of your life angry, looking for vengeance." He subtly glanced at his watch and reached for Evelyn's hand. "Your mom would want you to be happy. Honor her life." Will and Evelyn interlaced their fingers and squeezed each other's hands tightly.

Lydia stared at them, silent for several seconds. Then she opened her mouth and let out a loud cackle. "You think you know my mother better than I do?" She laughed again. "*Honor her life?* Why should I honor someone who obviously never told me the whole truth once? Who kept so many secrets it destroyed everyone around her and ripped our family apart?"

Without waiting for a response, Lydia lunged in Will's direction and snatched the gun from the end table, then whipped around, pointing it at Evelyn and Will, her finger on the trigger once again.

Evelyn was still clutching Will's arm, and she flinched as she anticipated the impact of the bullet headed her way, but instead the bright white light swallowed her again.

When she opened her eyes, she and Will were on the sofa in her apartment and Thomas was standing over them, Cecil's coat in hand.

"Thomas!" She let go of Will's hand and jumped up to embrace him, her gratitude overwhelming her. "You brought us back just in time!" She was panting from the panic of the ordeal. "I thought she was going to kill us!"

He pulled away from her, still holding her shoulders, his eyes wide. "Who?"

"Lydia! Caroline's daughter! She thinks Will killed Caroline! She came to his place with a gun!"

Thomas looked at Will, for the first time acknowledging that he was back in this timeline in spite of their original plans. He turned his attention back to Evelyn. "Thank goodness you're all right!" He hugged Evelyn again, genuinely thankful she'd made it back in one piece.

When he let her go, Evelyn turned to look at Will, who was still seated on the sofa with his head in his hands. "Will, are you all right?"

He didn't look up. "How do I get back there *without* bringing you with me?"

"What?"

He lifted his head. "How do I get back to the other timeline where I belong without you accompanying me? It's not safe and I won't put you in harm's way again. What if Lydia is still waiting for me when I go back next time?"

Evelyn wasn't sure how to answer. To her knowledge, it wasn't possible for him to travel back without a dreamer with him. And she was the only living dreamer they knew. She didn't even want to get into how weak her body was feeling after the trip she'd just taken to the other timeline and back with Will in tow. "I think I have to go with you," she said. "I don't think there is another way."

An uncomfortable silence blanketed the room. Evelyn was certain Thomas wasn't thrilled that he was in this situation for the second time, and she once again found herself stuck between her two loves.

Chapter 36
1922

Thomas had gone to Holstead's house and brought the doctor back to Evelyn's apartment in a cab. Holstead was the only person who could help figure out how to get Will back to 2006 once and for all without risking her safety.

In Evelyn's living room, the doctor paced back and forth as he spoke out loud. "There are several factors to consider. First, Will can't go back without a dreamer, and we only have one of those." He gestured toward Evelyn. "Then, we must consider that Evelyn has been back and forth across worlds multiple times just this week alone. If Fletch's research is correct, no dreamer can withstand that much traveling. Not even Evelyn. Another trip back and forth, especially transporting someone else with her, could be detrimental to her health. Even fatal."

"Are you saying there's no safe way to return him to his own timeline?" Thomas was doing a poor job concealing his irritation.

"I'm saying it would be risky in many ways to try, and entirely unpredictable. Since no dreamer has ever been known to have the amount of power Evelyn does, it's hard to say what her limits are. It's also difficult to quantify how all this traveling across timelines might affect Will. He isn't a dreamer. His body and mind may not withstand as much back and forth as Evelyn's can. Don't forget the state of the cork."

Evelyn processed the information until her mind settled on the obvious answer. "So we're both safer staying put?"

Holstead nodded.

"How long?" Will asked. "When will it be safe to travel again?"

"It's impossible to say." Holstead shrugged. "Like I said, these are uncharted waters as far as Fletch's research goes." He looked around the room, clearly aware of the love triangle that was unfolding in front of him. "The romantic and emotional implications aside, I would advise no more traveling for at least a few days, if not more."

"A few days?" Will's head shot up. "I can't miss a few days of work! I'll get fired."

"It's better than being shot to death," Evelyn sharply pointed out. She softened her tone. "If you go back now, Lydia could be waiting for you when you get there."

Holstead interjected. "I'll go through the files again and see if there's some other way. Maybe I've missed something, but I doubt I have."

"Thank you," Evelyn said, putting her hand on his shoulder. She couldn't do any of this without help, and she hoped Holstead knew how much she appreciated him.

"I should get back before Mrs. Brooks gets worried," Holstead said.

"I'll walk you home." Thomas typically walked the older man home when Mrs. Brooks wasn't around to make sure he got there safely.

"I'll be right back. Don't go anywhere." He looked at Evelyn as if to warn her not to time travel while he was gone.

"I'll see you when you get back," she assured him, squeezing his hand.

Thomas shot Will with a warning look as well. "I'll only be gone a few minutes."

As Thomas and Holstead walked the few blocks to the doctor's house, Thomas was deep in thought.

"It's not easy, is it?"

Thomas looked up. "I'm not sure what you mean."

"Seeing them together. It must be eating at you."

Thomas sighed. "It's not ideal."

Holstead paused, and Thomas wondered what he was trying to find the right words to say. Whatever it was, Thomas was sure it would cause him more anguish. Finally, Holstead spoke again. "I realize this isn't what you want to hear, but I feel I should warn you," he began.

Thomas turned his head to look at Holstead, his pulse quickening in anticipation of whatever bad news was imminent.

Holstead explained. "Based on everything I've read in the research files and everything I know about the dreams and the flashes, there is a distinct possibility that Will could be here for some time."

"Some time?" Thomas stopped walking. "How long?"

Holstead stopped and turned to face Thomas. He inhaled deeply and let out a long, slow breath before he answered. "I still have some research to do, but Will probably won't be able to get back to his own timeline. Ever."

The news took the air from Thomas's lungs for a moment. His face paled as he came to grips with the significance of it all. "I see."

Holstead patted him on the back reassuringly. "You'll all make it right, somehow."

Thomas shook his head slowly, peering into the traffic passing by on the street. "He deserves her, anyway."

"What do you mean? Don't give up yet!" Holstead gripped Thomas's shoulder. "She may still choose you!"

Thomas scoffed. "She shouldn't."

"Why ever not? You're a wonderful match for her!"

"Never mind." Thomas began walking again, and Holstead sped to catch up. Thomas changed the subject. "So what happens if we try to get him back to 2006 again?"

"I believe it would likely be disastrous. Evelyn might not survive it. And Will surely wouldn't. The cork all but confirmed he has a very limited capacity to travel back and forth. I would venture to say he's expended all his visits to the other timeline after this last little adventure. It's a wonder he isn't already hurt."

"So I have two choices. I can allow Evelyn to risk her own safety and possibly kill Will in the process of trying to kick him out of this timeline, and she would *never* forgive me for hurting him. Or, I can accept that he's here for good, and there's nothing I can do to keep the love of my life from running straight into his arms."

Holstead winced. "I don't envy your position, but surely you don't think it would be that easy for Evelyn to abandon you like that? Not after everything you two have been through together already."

"Like I said before. She would be better off. I'm not all I'm cracked up to be."

"Whatever it is you're worried about, I'm sure Evelyn doesn't love you any less for it."

Thomas laughed sarcastically. "That makes one of us."

They had finally reached Holstead's house, and Thomas bid the doctor a good day before he headed back to Evelyn's place. He had nervous butterflies in his stomach as he pictured how this would all take shape. Evelyn would never stop thinking about Will no matter which timeline he was in, and if he were here, within reach, Thomas could never live with himself for keeping them apart. Or live with a wife he knew really wanted someone else and from whom he'd kept major secrets. In the end, he wanted Evelyn's happiness over anything. Ideally he would be part of that happiness, but deep down he knew he was going to lose her, and piece by piece, it was breaking him.

Chapter 37
1922

Evelyn met Thomas at the door when he arrived back at her apartment. His jaw was tight, and he had little to say. He was trying to appear unbothered, but Evelyn knew him better. She sympathized with him and the difficult position he was in, but she hoped he could bear it all for a little longer until they figured it out.

The threesome sat in Evelyn's living room, another awkward silence crowding the space. Finally, Will spoke up. "If I have to be in this timeline for a few days, maybe it would be best if I found somewhere else to stay."

Evelyn snapped her head toward him, shocked. "Why?"

"It's not fair to your relationship. I wouldn't want me here if I were in Thomas's position."

Thomas raised his eyebrows and said nothing.

Evelyn sat up straight in her seat. "But there's nowhere else to go!" she cried, doing a shoddy job of hiding her staunch objection to his leaving. "Where would you stay if not here?"

Will looked at Thomas, assuming he would think of something if he wanted them apart badly enough.

Thomas sighed. "My mother is going out of town to visit her cousins in the Hamptons, but not until tomorrow. After she's gone you could stay at my place."

Evelyn flinched at the idea. "Won't that be . . . uncomfortable?" She glanced back and forth between the two men.

"We'll make do," Thomas said quickly.

"I think that's best, don't you?" Will asked Evelyn. She clenched her fists, trying to stuff down her irritation in spite of knowing he was right. She still hadn't told Thomas about the kisses she and Will had shared. She'd wait until the moment was right before she told him. There was no sense making an already uncomfortable situation totally unbearable. Especially for Will, who hadn't asked to be here. Silently, she'd hoped she could spend more time with him while he was. Her nerves were shot, and she wanted to scream the truth to Thomas. Tell him how she really felt. But she couldn't break him yet. She loved him, too. The fact that he was even still sitting here told her how much he loved her back.

"Yes, I suppose that's the best thing." Her voice fell as she said it. She couldn't help it.

"What about tonight?" Will asked. "Do you think I could stay at Doctor Holstead's until tomorrow?"

Evelyn shrugged. "I doubt it. It's a small house. I don't think there's a spare room."

"I'm not sure there's any alternative tonight." Thomas's shoulders slumped a bit. He sounded defeated. "You'll have to stay here, Will."

Evelyn's stomach flipped as it always had for Will. Spending some time alone with him—even just to talk—was all she wanted. If this was their last visit across timelines, she wanted more than surface-level group conversations with Thomas around. She wanted to speak to Will from her heart. And she wanted him to tell her all the things that were inside his.

"How many days does Holstead think it will take to get an answer about how I can get back?" Will asked.

Thomas opened his mouth to say something, then closed it again.

"What's wrong?" Evelyn could read the tension on his face. There was something he wasn't telling her. "Thomas, what did Holstead say?"

He rubbed his face with both hands as he prepared himself to deliver the news. He exhaled sharply. "Holstead seems to think Will might be stuck here."

"Stuck?" Will straightened up in his seat. "For how long?"

Thomas swallowed and looked at Evelyn as he uttered the word he clearly dreaded putting into the universe. "Forever."

A stunned silence was the only reaction Evelyn and Will could muster. She licked her lips slowly as she processed what Thomas had just said, but one thing was clear as day: if Will was going to be in this timeline forever, Evelyn wanted to be with him. She couldn't say that in front of Thomas, and Will would have a lot of adjustments to make if he was going to be stuck here in the 1920s with her. She would have to help him along. What would that mean for Thomas? It was all too much to come to terms with in an instant.

"I had the same reaction," Thomas said. "Holstead says Evelyn doesn't have much more traveling in her, if any. At least not without hurting herself." He looked at Will. "He thinks the cork is a harbinger of what would happen to you if you tried to go again. And you can't go without her."

Will closed his eyes and inhaled long and hard, deep in thought. Finally, he exhaled and opened his eyes. "I never meant to show up here and upend your life." He glanced at Evelyn. "Your relationship."

Thomas scoffed. "I think if we're all being honest, you've always been here."

Evelyn jumped up from her seat. "Thomas, let's not discuss this now." She crossed the room to join him, gently touching his arm. "We'll talk in private. Later."

Thomas chuckled softly, a forced grin on his face. "Of course. We'll talk later."

Evelyn was concerned at the way his mood was shifting, and she wasn't looking forward to their impending private conversation. She pitied his difficult position, but she still wanted to support and welcome Will. Pleasing both men at the same time was proving more impossible than she'd ever imagined.

Thomas headed for the door.

"Where are you going?" Evelyn walked after him, afraid he wasn't planning on coming back.

He pulled on his coat. "I suppose if our guest is going to be here a while, he'll need some more clothing. I'm going to get him an outfit for tomorrow and some pajamas for this evening."

Evelyn arched her brow, impressed. It touched her that even in what was probably one of the toughest circumstances he'd ever faced, he was still willing to go the extra mile to make her happy and to fulfill any emergent needs. She wished he'd been this way in their fights about his work and the wedding. She rushed over to the door before he stepped out and squeezed his forearm.

"Thank you."

He gazed down into her eyes for a few seconds. "I'll be back soon." He opened the front door and disappeared, leaving Evelyn and Will alone again.

It didn't escape Evelyn that Thomas hadn't bothered to give her a kiss on the cheek or given her any other sign of his affection before he left. She couldn't blame him.

Evelyn went to the sofa and sat next to Will, putting her hand on his knee. "Are you all right?" She was worried about him. The revelation that he may have to give up his entire life for one he knew nothing about was enormous, and she wasn't sure how he would handle it.

He stared straight ahead, lost in thought. "I've been sitting here trying to think of what I would be giving up there." Evelyn took his hand, holding it gently as she waited for him to go on. He scoffed. "The sad truth is, I have nothing there to lose. Without you and my mom, I have *nothing* in that life worth going back to." His chin was quivering.

The last time Evelyn had seen him cry was the night she'd died in his arms in 2003. This was breaking her heart in a completely different way. "No, Will, don't say that."

"It's true! All I have is an apartment I never decorated, a job I'm barely clinging to, and some staff at a dive bar who might miss the revenue. I've been on autopilot every day since my mom died. Just going through the motions. Doing everything I can to forget the fact that I have no one to live for. That there's nothing special about my life. Nothing that makes a tangible difference. I used to take care of my mom. I used to have you. Now, I'm just a body. My mind has been somewhere else for a long time. Here."

Her mouth went dry, and she took a shaky breath. "I don't know what to say."

He turned in his seat to face her. His eyes were intense, even through the moisture that was forming in them. "Tell me you want me."

"What?"

"Evelyn, it's killing me to see you with Thomas! He loves you, I know that. But *not* the way I do!" He stopped talking and laced his fingers behind his head as he looked up at the ceiling, exasperated. "I'm sorry. I shouldn't have said that. I just . . . know you."

She focused her gaze on her hands, which were now clasped so tight her knuckles were white. She realized she was still wearing her engagement ring. "It's complicated."

"I know! I know it is." He reached over and touched her face, gently turning it toward him. "Just tell me what you really want."

She leaned forward and rested her forehead on his. "Why do things always have to be so hard for you and me?"

He closed his eyes. "Because what we have is worth it."

They sat like that for a few seconds, unsure how to move forward knowing what Will had just said was the unadulterated truth. Their love was worth every bit of hardship and heartbreak.

Finally, she pulled back and sat up straight. "I know you're right. I just don't want to break Thomas's heart. He's such a good man, and he doesn't deserve it." She paused, scared to say the next part out loud. "But the truth is, if you're here, in this world, with me, I could never marry him or love him with my whole heart." She thought about it for a moment. "If I'm being completely honest, I'm not sure I ever *have* given him my whole heart. Part of it was always still with you, in the other life. And he's always known it."

Neither of them said anything for a while. They just sat, contemplating how much both their lives could be about to change.

Will spoke first. "What are we going to do?"

Evelyn stood and walked slowly around the room, thinking. She had no answer. Her heart was palpitating wildly at the idea that everything she'd ever really wanted with Will could become a reality soon, in spite of how hard it would be to get there. She could have a second chance with him. The repercussions of such a choice weren't lost on her. In order to go after what she truly desired, she'd have to leave a brokenhearted Thomas in her wake, and that was the very last thing she'd ever wanted to do. Before she could summon a reply, Thomas's keys jingled outside the doorway. He was back already.

Thomas exhaled when he walked in, relieved to see Evelyn and Will on opposite sides of the room. He placed his bag on the coffee table in front of Will. "Here's everything you should need to get you through a couple of days, at least. Depending how long you're around, we might have to go and buy you some more clothes."

Will stood and reached out to shake Thomas's hand. "Thank you."

Thomas hesitated, then took Will's hand, nodding. "Maybe this time, don't lose my suit in an alternate timeline." They all laughed nervously, relieved that someone had brought some levity to this situation.

Evelyn was unsure how to proceed. She needed more time to talk to Will alone, but she also desperately wanted to make Thomas feel better. His discomfort was obvious in spite of his good graces, and it was killing her to see how much she was already hurting him, and she hadn't even delivered the final blow yet. "Shall I make us something to eat?" she asked. "It's getting late."

"I'm afraid I have to get back home to help my mother prepare for her trip out east." Thomas looked Will in the eye as he spoke. "I'll come back as early as I can tomorrow morning after she leaves and we can get Will over to my place." Thomas was clearly eager to get Will out of Evelyn's apartment and under his own watchful eye.

"Are you sure you can't come back tonight?" Evelyn asked, half intending to make Thomas feel wanted, and half trying to confirm whether she could expect to have more time to talk to Will.

"I'm afraid not," he said. "Mother is leaving early in the morning, and she'll need my assistance getting her bags out to the car when it arrives."

It genuinely did touch Evelyn's heart how dedicated Thomas was to helping his mother. It dawned on her that it was something he and Will had in common. "I'll see you in the morning."

Thomas gave Will one last glare before he headed for the door, this time stopping to kiss Evelyn on the cheek on his way out. Making sure Will couldn't hear, he leaned down and whispered close to her ear, "You know how much I love you."

"I love you, too," she murmured back. She meant it, even if she had to break his heart soon.

Chapter 38

1922

With the entire night ahead of them now that Thomas had departed, an electricity buzzed between Evelyn and Will that couldn't be ignored. She wanted so much to be loyal to Thomas in spite of their engagement hiatus until she could find the right time to end things with him, but the animal magnetism that drew her to Will was unlike anything she'd ever had with Thomas. She forced herself to fight off her urges. In spite of the way she wanted Will, she also had some important things to discuss with him.

Will had unpacked the bag Thomas brought over and laid out the clothes on the armchair. He was stuffing a spare pillow into a pillowcase while Evelyn fixed a makeshift bed for him on the sofa. She secretly wished he wouldn't end up using it. She would love nothing more than another night lying blissfully in his arms. She glanced up at him and noticed he looked crestfallen. "Are you all right?" She straightened up and came over to him, taking the pillow from his hands and putting it on the sofa. "Do you want to talk?"

Staring off into the distance, he said quietly, "I just thought of one thing I don't want to leave in my other life." He shook his head. "But it's too late now."

"Will, what is it?"

He swallowed. "My mom's ashes."

The words pierced her heart. Of course he'd want the urn. It was all he had left of his mother. "Oh, Will. I hadn't thought of that. I'm so sorry." She sat on the sofa now made up into a bed. "I can't imagine how much you must miss her. You've already been through so much, and now I've ripped your life away from you and brought you here."

He sat next to her. "I don't even care about the rest of it, though. I just miss her so much, Evelyn. I can't bear the thought of her remains being tossed away once I've gone missing in the other timeline. She deserves more than that." He choked up. Evelyn took his hand and held it firmly. She had no words that would make it better. Silently, she vowed to find a way to get the urn for him, no matter the toll it took. If he was going to sacrifice everything to be here, in this life with her, the very least she could do was reunite him with his mother's remains.

Later that night, with Will fast asleep on Evelyn's living room sofa, she tossed and turned in the bedroom. She was ridden with guilt over Lynn's ashes and desperate to get back to 2006 and bring the urn back for him. Holstead had told Thomas she shouldn't travel again, and while Evelyn was terrified she'd run into Lydia if she returned to the other timeline, it was a chance she was willing to take. New York was a big place, and the odds of seeing Lydia were slim.

She climbed out of bed and quietly got dressed. A chill ran up her spine at the idea of going back to 2006 in spite of the risks, but this was the only way she could help Will. He and Thomas would never let her try if they knew. They would be too concerned for her health, and this was something she needed to do for Will. Caroline had said she felt the energy draining from her, and knew when she was done traveling, but Evelyn's energy wasn't depleted yet. Not fully. Whatever she had left, she was willing to use it for this worthy cause.

Dressed, she crept into the living room, careful not to wake Will. She checked to make sure he was sound asleep and wouldn't catch her traveling. He stirred when she got near but quickly pulled the covers tighter around himself and settled. She returned to her bedroom and retrieved her alarm clock from the nightstand. It was important for her to be able to get back to this timeline without the help of another person this time. Her closet was packed tight with clothes, but she crouched down and wedged herself inside against the hanging garments until she could close the door. She hoped it would be enough to stop the noise from the alarm from waking Will. She took a deep breath, closed her eyes, and draped Cecil's coat over herself.

The glaring light made her wince, telling her it had worked. After a few seconds in the blinding white, she was, once again, in Will's living room, clad in her prohibition-era clothing.

She immediately headed for the mantle where the urn sat. The plaque bearing Lynn Jenkins's name glinted in the moonlight shining through the window. She picked up the urn and held it close to her. Halfway across the living room and back to the front door, a familiar voice stopped her in her tracks.

"Evelyn?"

She was numb.

In the bedroom doorway stood her best friend. Her chosen family. The only person besides Will who had truly ever understood her. She wanted to speak, but the words were caught in her throat.

"No. No, I have to be dreaming. This isn't possible." Cammie was rubbing her eyes as she spoke to herself. "Ghosts aren't real. This isn't happening."

Evelyn wasn't sure whether she was about to burst into tears or into a fit of elated laughter. "It's real." She could barely manage more than a whisper. "It's real, Cammie."

Cammie stared across the room at what she was certain was a hallucination. "I'm desperate for that to be true, but it's impossible. I'm dreaming." Her breath was unsteady as she walked a few steps toward Evelyn, squinting to verify she wasn't envisioning things that weren't actually there. When she was a few feet away, she stopped.

Evelyn almost made a move toward her but didn't want to scare her friend. "Cam, I'm going to come over to you, okay?"

Cammie nodded, her eyes wide. Evelyn slowly walked across the room to her and stopped about an arm's length away.

After a few tense seconds, Cammie reached out her hand and gently touched Evelyn's upper arm. She gasped and pulled her hand back when her fingers met a real, solid person. She couldn't blink.

Evelyn was motionless. She was afraid that any sudden movement would send her best friend running from the apartment.

After all, Cammie had no idea she was still alive in another timeline, let alone that she'd ever be able to see Evelyn again. "I know this is scary, but I can explain it. Please believe me. It's really me."

Cammie took a few steps backward, shaking her head and laughing in disbelief. "This is too much." She turned and started toward the door to leave.

"Please don't go!" Evelyn was desperate to keep Cammie here so she could talk to her one last time and explain everything.

Cammie froze. After a few seconds, she turned back around to face Evelyn. She slowly walked toward the couch and sat down, speaking out loud to herself. "Okay. Whether this is real or not, it's a once-in-a-lifetime opportunity. I'm pretty sure I'm losing it, but here goes nothing."

Evelyn sighed in relief. She moved toward the couch to sit down next to Cammie. "Is it okay if I sit with you?"

Cammie rolled her eyes and motioned to the empty seat. "Sitting on couches with ghosts! Sure, why not?"

"I'm not a ghost, Cam."

"Then what exactly *are* you? This isn't normal!"

"I know."

"How are you here? Did you fake your death? Are you in the witness protection program? What is going *on*?" Cammie's brain was filing through all the possibilities faster than she could verbalize them.

"No! It's a long story."

"I've got time."

Evelyn ran her hands over her face, unsure how to squeeze a lifetime of secrets into a brief summation. "I'll try and explain the best I can. And before I start, I need you to set a timer for twenty-five minutes, because that's about how much time I have left here."

Cammie stared at her, willing her to begin explaining this unfathomable situation. She soon complied, setting the timer on her phone. Evelyn finally started talking, confessing everything she'd ever kept from her best friend about the dreams and time traveling. She explained the flashes and told Cammie about Lydia. And finally, how she'd accidentally transported Will into another timeline with her. Cammie took it all in without a word. Evelyn eventually got to the end of the story and Cammie's expression hadn't changed a bit the entire time. Evelyn couldn't tell whether she believed it or not. After a long silence, Cammie stood up. Evelyn stood as well, unsure of what to expect next. Cammie walked in a slow, deliberate circle around Evelyn, looking her up and down, assessing whether she should buy the story. Evelyn wrung her hands, wishing fervently for Cammie to believe her. Finally, Cammie stopped and stood in front of Evelyn, looking her directly in the eye, studying her.

Moments later, Cammie finally spoke. "I hate those clothes."

Evelyn burst into simultaneous laughter and tears of joy as the two best friends embraced in a reunion they'd never thought possible. When they'd finally gotten ahold of themselves, they sat back down on the couch. Cammie wiped her face dry. "You have to leave again, don't you?"

Evelyn lowered her eyes. "I'm afraid so. It's not good for me to be here too long."

"Is Will going to stay with you?"

"It's hard to say. Right now I don't know how to get him back here, and Holstead doesn't seem to think I could do it without hurting Will or myself."

Cammie bit her lower lip. Evelyn knew something was bothering her. Cammie always chewed her lip when she had something she wanted to get off her chest.

"What is it?"

"I never meant for anything to happen between me and Will. I'm the worst friend ever. I'm so, so sorry."

"Cam, don't apologize. You didn't do anything wrong."

"Then why do I feel so guilty?"

"You couldn't have known I'd be back."

"It doesn't matter! Will was never mine to have. I should have respected what you two had. I just—" She swallowed. "I just missed you so much, and I felt bad for him. My emotions ran away with me, and I let them. Will and I aren't a match. We all know it. He was only ever meant to be with you, Ev. And now I guess he can be. This is the way it's supposed to be."

"I wish there was a way you and I could hang out sometimes. Or at least write to each other. I hate it that I don't know if I'll see you again."

"I'm still really grateful we got this time."

"Me too." Evelyn squeezed her friend's hand. "What are you doing here, anyway? I wasn't expecting anyone to be in Will's apartment."

"I've been trying to get in touch with Will for two days. I just wanted to make sure he was okay. He was in my hospital a few days ago. He didn't get back to me and I was concerned, so I came over on my way home from work to check on him."

Evelyn's heart warmed. "You really did take care of him for me, didn't you?"

"I tried."

"Thank you." Evelyn was struggling to find the right words, and time was ticking away. "I don't want to leave you again."

Cammie sputtered through tears. "I wish you could stay!"

They hugged again. Evelyn pulled away, her hands on Cammie's shoulders. "I love you, you know. You're not just my best friend. You're my sister. If I can ever come back safely and see you, I swear I'll be here in an instant."

"You'd better." Cammie could barely speak. "I miss you so much, Ev."

"I miss you, too. And I'm so proud of you. You're living your dream like I always knew you would."

"You were supposed to be here to see it."

"I'm here now. And I see it. I see you."

"I can't believe you're not gone. Like, you're still out there somewhere, alive and well."

"I'm out there. Somewhere. And I'll always be rooting for you from wherever that is."

"I'm rooting for you and Will, too." A small smile came across Cammie's face. "I can see why you were head over heels for him. He really is your perfect match."

A twinge of sadness and guilt hit Evelyn's chest. Will *was* her perfect match, which didn't leave much room for Thomas. The thought of her dueling lovers in 1922 reminded her that she needed to get back there before Will woke up. She glanced at the timer on the phone. "In a few minutes I'm going to have to go back there."

Together for the first time in years, and possibly for the last time in their lives, they hugged tightly as they prepared to say what might be their final goodbye.

"So how does this work? You just kinda . . . vanish into thin air?"

"Pretty much," Evelyn said, picking up the urn. "An alarm clock in the other timeline will go off and jolt me out of this daydream, and I'll be back there."

"You know, you've done a lot of things that surprised me over the years, but this definitely tops the list."

Evelyn laughed. "I think I miss your humor most of all," she confessed. "No one in the other life makes me laugh the way you do."

Cammie took Evelyn's free hand and squeezed it. "And no one here gets me the way you do."

"I wish you could come with me." Evelyn's voice broke as she said it.

"Oh, Ev. We both know I'd never survive the prohibition era without landing in jail."

They laughed again, and Evelyn's eyes welled with more tears. She would give anything for more time with Cammie. "I have no idea how to say goodbye to you."

"Then don't say it. You're gonna figure out a way to get back here one day. I know you."

They pulled each other close and embraced one last time before Evelyn had to go. She'd never had a real sister, but she imagined this is what saying goodbye to one would feel like. Heart-wrenching.

"I guess it's time," she said, clutching the urn close to her body.

Cammie sniffed. "I feel like I'm dreaming. I never thought I'd get to see you again. I'm so happy. And so sad at the same time." She grabbed Evelyn's shoulders. "I love you, BFF."

"I am so glad I got to see you and tell you the truth. Thank you for believing me."

"Always."

"I love you, too."

Cammie stepped back to give Evelyn some space. "See you soon?"

"As soon as possible." Evelyn gripped the urn and smiled at her friend one last time before the white light consumed her and took her home.

Chapter 39

1922

Evelyn scrambled out of the closet, trying to keep quiet in hopes that Will would still be asleep. She tucked the urn away in her dresser and went into the living room to check on him. When she approached the sofa, she examined his sleeping figure silhouetted in the moonlight. His steady breathing told her she'd made it back before he'd even realized she was gone.

Her body was shaky and her mind a bit blurry from the journey to 2006. She had to get some rest to recover. She'd have to appear fine in the morning if no one was to know she'd traveled.

She stood next to Will and gazed down at him as he slept, his mind probably a million miles away. It was almost too good to be true that he might end up in her timeline, but she couldn't let go of the guilt that was persistently hanging over her for inadvertently bringing him here. She hoped the urn would help a little.

Will shifted positions, and Evelyn held her breath, waiting to see if he would wake up. When she was satisfied he wasn't going to, she bent over and kissed him so softly on the forehead she wasn't sure she'd actually touched him at all. She simply couldn't deny that his mere presence made her pulse race and fulfilled her soul. She'd never loved anyone so much, and the way her heart swelled for him made her surer than ever that she was going to have to break a heart—and soon.

She'd think about it in the morning. Exhausted, Evelyn tiptoed back into her bedroom and slipped out of her street clothes. Dressed in her nightgown, she got into her bed and pulled the covers up to her chin. She knew she shouldn't, but she couldn't help thinking how much she wished Will was sleeping in the bed next to her. She finally drifted off, content for now just to have him in the same timeline.

Evelyn awoke the next morning to the sound of dishes clanging in her kitchen. She made her way out of the bedroom to see what Will was doing. A chuckle escaped her at the sight of him bent over, trying to figure out the coal stove. "This is why I don't cook much."

He shot up, then softened and smiled when he laid eyes on her. "I guess I have a few things to learn if I'm stuck in this timeline, huh?"

"I don't want you to feel stuck."

"I didn't mean it like that." He walked toward her. "You know there's nowhere I'd rather be."

Butterflies swarmed in her stomach. Everything about being with him was so effortlessly right. She said nothing, her heart beating faster just from his closeness. Suddenly she remembered the urn. "I have something for you."

Before he could respond, a knock sounded at the door. Thomas had arrived. Evelyn glanced at Will before she opened it. She was slightly annoyed that their time alone had ended and that Thomas had come to swoop Will away from her so soon. She had to admit she'd probably do the same thing in Thomas's position, but still, waking up with Will in her apartment had felt so natural. Like Cammie said, this is how things were supposed to be, and in her heart, Evelyn knew it.

Thomas walked in, his coat draped over his arm. He kissed Evelyn on the cheek. "Good morning."

"Good morning. Did your mother get off on her trip all right?"

"After a bit of a scuffle over a missing hat, yes." He grinned. "How was your night?" He looked at Will as he said it.

"Uneventful," Will replied. "I was exhausted after everything that happened the last couple of days. I just woke up, actually."

Thomas eyed them both, sizing up whether that was the whole truth. "I have to go to the office today, but I thought I'd come and take Will over to my house first."

Evelyn fought off a grimace. She wasn't ready for Will to go. "Yes, good idea," she said, disguising her disappointment. "I should get dressed." She hurried into her bedroom and changed back into the clothes she'd worn the night before when she'd secretly popped into the next millennium to collect Lynn Jenkins's ashes. She'd have to figure out how to get the urn to Will some other time. She couldn't let Thomas find out she'd traveled when he'd trusted her not to. Again.

Voices filtered into the bedroom from the living room. The men were making small talk, both probably hoping she would return sooner rather than later. She peeked around the doorframe to see how they were getting on.

"What kind of practice are you opening?" Will asked as he pulled the suspenders on his borrowed pants over his shoulders, preparing to venture outside in disguise.

"Psychotherapy," Thomas answered proudly. "It's not a very popular field yet and just gaining steam, but getting in on the ground floor will hopefully be an asset."

"It will, trust me."

"How do you . . . ah. Of course." Will had the advantage of literally knowing what the distant future held. Evelyn had often used the same argument to reassure Thomas when he'd been discouraged about starting his business.

"If you need any help with anything, let me know," Will offered sincerely. "I don't know the medical side of things, but I can help with construction. Maybe even answer some more general questions you might have about psychology in the future."

As awkward as it was, Evelyn had to admit it wasn't a bad idea. Will had minored in psychology, after all. Having the upper hand when it came to planning ahead would certainly be helpful to Thomas as far as deciding what direction to take his business. Still, Thomas would never be comfortable working alongside the man who had a vise grip on Evelyn's heart. Thomas paused, and Evelyn wondered if he was having the same train of thought. As expected, he politely dismissed Will's offer. "Thank you. I'll let you know if I think of anything."

She finished dressing for the day and emerged from the bedroom. The sight of her two men, both dressed in their 1922 clothing, standing beside each other in the same room and the same timeline, was both wildly exciting and terrifying. She'd always wished she could be back with Will, but she'd never imagined she'd have to give up Thomas to make that wish come true. She'd always assumed the universe would decide for her. A few weeks ago, she thought it already had. "Are we ready?"

The trio quickly walked a few blocks to Thomas's house. Will was still getting used to this version of the city and gaped at the automobiles, the roads, the prices advertised in the shop windows, and more. Evelyn found it endearing that he was taking everything in stride. It occurred to her that if he didn't have her, he probably wouldn't be. She vowed to do everything in her power to make his transition into this life as seamless as possible, knowing it would be a delicate dance to help Will and keep Thomas happy at the same time until she finally had her talk with Thomas.

When they arrived at the house, Thomas showed Will to the guest room, where just a few nights prior, Caroline Huber had visited Evelyn. Her chest tightened when she thought about Caroline.

"I have to get to work." Thomas was already halfway out the door. "Sorry to rush everyone, but I'm running late. I need to let the builders into the office."

Evelyn joined him, looking back at Will. "What should Will do all day?"

"He can do anything he likes! I've sent the cook home while my mother is away, so there's no one here." He motioned for Will to follow him down the hall. "There's a library there, and a sitting room down that way. Kitchen is stocked, so please help yourself to anything."

"Thank you," Will said, genuinely appreciative. "You didn't have to do any of this for me."

"It's nothing." Thomas forced a smile. "I must get going. Evelyn?" He held out his arm, and she took it. The group made their way to the front door.

"I should be home around five o'clock," Thomas said to Will. "Like I said, make yourself at home."

"I'll come by at about five as well." Evelyn turned to Will. "Are you going to be okay until then?"

"Don't worry." He smiled at her, and her heart skipped a beat.

"We'll see you later," she called to him as she and Thomas exited the house. Will closed the door, and Thomas and Evelyn descended the outside steps to the sidewalk. They were headed in separate directions, so they stopped to say their goodbyes.

"I hope you won't take it the wrong way when I ask that you please wait to come back to the house until after I'm home from work," Thomas said. "I don't mean to imply anything, it's just . . . uncomfortable. For me."

She looked at the ground. His discomfort wasn't unfounded. She had kissed Will a few times already, and he'd even slept in her bed one night. They hadn't done anything untoward, but she knew kissing would be enough to tear Thomas apart, and it was killing her that no matter how long she dragged it out or how many secrets she kept, breaking his heart was inevitable. "I understand," she said as confidently as she could. "I'll see you back here at five." She raised up on her toes to kiss him before she turned and headed home. She couldn't keep up this show much longer.

Chapter 40

1922

Later that morning, outside Thomas's house, Evelyn scolded herself for coming back so soon and breaking her word to Thomas. He had specifically asked her not to come back until he was home from work, but she was dying to get the urn to Will. She was sure he would want to have it with him. She climbed the steps, the urn safely in her bag, ready to reunite Lynn Jenkins with her son.

"Evelyn?"

She froze. *Thomas.*

"What are you doing back here? I thought we said not until five?"

She spun around on her heel, red-faced at being caught. "I—" She could barely form a sentence. "Will left something at my apartment."

Thomas sneered. "Something so important he couldn't wait until five o'clock to have it?"

She looked down, embarrassed. "It's nothing."

He waited to see if she would change her mind and come clean. She didn't. "I see."

"You see what?" Evelyn was nervous he was about to explode, and she really couldn't blame him.

"I'm just starting to wonder if there's a lot more you don't tell me. It seems like I'm uncovering secret after secret, and every time, it's got something to do with him." He paused, giving her a chance to defend herself.

She was quiet for a long time before she finally spoke. "You're right." She reached into her bag and pulled out the urn. "It's his mother."

Thomas read the inscription. He drew a sharp breath, and the disappointment and hurt were written all over his face as he pieced together what she'd done. "He didn't bring this here with him, did he?"

Evelyn put the urn back in her bag and hung her head. "No."

"What am I supposed to do here, Evelyn?"

"I don't know." It was barely a whisper. She had a painful lump in her throat. She wished he could fully understand that her own position was even more complex to navigate than his.

He gazed at her for what seemed like an eternity, her mouth becoming drier with every second that passed. "I need to get back to the office. I forgot some papers." He rushed up the steps and disappeared inside, leaving her alone on the sidewalk. She stared at the closed door, her eyes moistening with tears. Turning to head for her apartment, she thought better of it and changed directions. She needed advice, and she could only think of one place to get it.

Soon, Evelyn knocked on Mariah's front door. Her birth mother welcomed her with a huge smile before she caught a glimpse of Evelyn's tear-stained face. "Come in, dear." She hustled Evelyn inside and closed the door. "What's the matter?" Mariah gasped when Evelyn fell into her arms, bawling.

Mariah stroked Evelyn's hair as she cried. "It's all right. Shhh. I'm here."

Evelyn finally caught her breath, still wrapped in Mariah's embrace. "I don't know what to do! I need help!"

Minutes later, Evelyn was seated comfortably across from Mariah in the small sitting room, dabbing her eyes with a handkerchief. Mariah placed her hand gently on Evelyn's knee. "Now, tell me. What's the matter?"

Evelyn explained how she'd accidentally brought Will into this timeline and described the ensuing relationship fallout. She began to tear up again when she got to the part where Thomas had walked away from her that afternoon. "He's been so patient and so understanding. So giving. And I make him feel like it's never enough." She sniffed and twisted the hanky in her hands.

"Maybe that's because it isn't."

Evelyn's head snapped up. "What?"

Mariah stood and joined Evelyn on the sofa. "If there's one thing I've learned about love, it's that the one you're truly meant to be with will make everyone else seem . . . wrong." She gazed ahead dreamily.

"Did you love someone other than your husband? My father?"

Mariah chuckled softly. "No. The version of Fletch that I met before he started studying the dreams was the greatest love of my life. After the adoption, I never saw him the same way. Even though Fletcher was here with me every day, I still missed the man he used to be. My soulmate."

Evelyn nodded in understanding. She could relate. "I'm scared of breaking Thomas's heart."

Mariah squeezed her hand. "I know. But don't break your own heart to protect his. He will be fine, you know."

"I don't even know for sure yet that Will is going to be in this timeline forever. What if I end things with Thomas and then something happens and Will is gone, and I'm left with nothing?"

"Then you'll hurt, and you'll get through it, and you'll go on. And you won't have nothing. I'll always be here."

"Thank you." Evelyn was grateful to have Mariah. She'd never been able to be completely open with anyone in this timeline about the dreams and all their romantic complexities the way she could with Mariah. It was a breath of fresh air and the soft landing Evelyn desperately needed amongst all the emotional unrest.

"It's actually really easy to choose, you know."

Evelyn furrowed her brow. "What do you mean?"

"It's simple. Ask yourself one question: would you ever forgive yourself if you didn't give the love of your life every chance you could?"

It took Evelyn a few seconds to ponder the question, but the answer was plain in her mind. She shook her head. "Never."

"I won't tell you what to do, but give it some thought. I'm always here if you need to talk it over."

Evelyn was quiet for a while. "Can Will stay here?" Mariah was taken aback at the question but considered it. Evelyn continued making her case. "It's just that staying at Thomas's must be so uncomfortable for them both, and Thomas won't want Will back at my place. If Will is here, they don't have to see each other as much."

"True," Mariah said. "Of course, I don't know him. But I trust that you wouldn't put me in harm's way."

"Will would never hurt you! Or anyone. He's the gentlest, kindest person I've ever known."

"If you trust him, I trust him."

"I do. With my life. And thank you. This means the world to me."

"It's the least I can do."

Chapter 41

1922

It was five o'clock and Evelyn was dreading seeing Thomas again after their fight, but she needed to get Will into Mariah's house and out of Thomas's as soon as possible, for all their sakes. She waited on the front steps for Thomas to come home.

He finally arrived, sighing when he saw her waiting for him. "I don't want to argue anymore," he said, going around her to unlock the door. "I know you're just here to see Will, so let's get this over with."

"No!" She grabbed his arm. He stopped and faced her on the doorstep, waiting for her to continue. "I'm not just here to see him. I wanted to talk to you. I think it would be best for all of us if Will stayed at Mariah's house until we've figured this out once and for all."

Thomas took a breath and considered the notion. "I can't say I hate the idea of him not being in *my* house."

"I know. It's just that it's my fault he's even in this timeline and now it's up to me to make it work."

He gazed down at her, directly into her eyes. "You know I can't share you. I need your whole heart. It has to be your whole heart, Evelyn."

She closed her eyes and nodded. He cupped her cheek in his hand.

They stood for a few moments. His love for her was real, and it was palpable. She desperately wished she could want only him, but the raw truth was her heart had always been split between two men, and one had the lion's share.

Eventually, he let go and put the key in the door. "We should go in. Will is probably bored out of his mind."

She followed him inside. She hated what she was doing to Thomas.

When they entered the house, Will met them in the hallway. The three stood, no one sure what to say.

Evelyn broke the unbearable silence. "Will, how would you feel about moving over to Mariah Fletcher's house for the time being?"

"Mariah Fletcher? As in your biological mother?"

"Yes. I went to see her today and asked if she'd mind having you stay with her for a while. Just until we sort everything out."

"I suppose that would be better for everyone involved." Will glanced at Thomas.

"I'm sure it would be nice for you to have some company during the day, as well," Thomas pointed out.

"So it's settled, then?" Both men nodded. "Good." Evelyn was relieved to have solved at least one problem.

"Speaking of sorting things out," Thomas interjected, "what exactly is our long-term plan here? How do we find out whether Will is stuck here permanently or not?"

Evelyn shrugged. "I suppose we need to talk to Holstead again. See if he's learned anything new from Fletch's files."

"I can't go tomorrow. I'm tied up with work all day," Thomas said.

Will chimed in. "We'll go." Evelyn raised her eyebrows, surprised he was so eager to learn whether he could go back to his timeline. Will caught her expression. "It must be awful for Thomas not to know what's going to happen. We should go as soon as we can. Give him some peace of mind."

Thomas dropped his jaw in surprise but didn't argue.

"All right," Evelyn agreed. "We'll talk to Holstead tomorrow." She was itching to get out of this tricky conversation. "We should get you over to Mariah's."

Will nodded in agreement. "I'll get packed."

A while later, the three arrived at Mariah's. Her eyes twinkled at the sight of Evelyn with her two loves. "Ah, I've been expecting you!" She ushered them all inside, trying to decipher which man was which.

"Mariah, this is Will Jenkins." Evelyn motioned toward him. "And this is Thomas." She put her hand on his arm. She hoped the small act would comfort him.

Mariah quickly glanced back and forth between Will and Thomas. "Of course," she said, smiling at Thomas. "I've heard such wonderful things about both of you from Evelyn."

"That's a relief." Thomas laughed, easing up a bit. Evelyn was impressed at Mariah's ability to soothe the male ego.

A few minutes later, Thomas and Evelyn were in the sitting room while Mariah showed Will where he'd be staying. The silence in the room was cumbersome, and Evelyn wanted badly to make him feel better somehow. She walked up behind him as he admired a painting on the wall and put her hand on his shoulder. He didn't turn his gaze. "I'm sorry I traveled to the other timeline without telling you," she said quietly. He didn't say anything, and his silence was starting to scare her. He usually had an answer for everything. "Thomas, I said I'm *sorry*!"

He kept staring forward at the painting. "Is there anything you won't do for him?"

"What?"

He finally turned to face her, her hand dropping from his shoulder.

"It's amazing to me the lengths you're willing to go for Will."

"Thomas, please don't do this here."

"No, really. You're willing to sacrifice anything for him. Even me."

"That's not true."

"Then tell me you'll choose me if he stays in this timeline."

Their faces were inches apart. Part of her was itching to just blurt out the truth, that she'd already chosen Will, but she couldn't do it. Not like this. He stared at her, his nostrils flaring as he waited for an answer.

Just then the door swung open and Mariah entered. Evelyn's distraught face immediately conveyed how badly she needed a lifeline. Thankfully, Mariah threw her one. "Evelyn, would you mind helping me get some refreshments ready?"

Thankful for the exit strategy, Evelyn relaxed her shoulders and agreed.

"Will should be back down shortly," Mariah said, glancing back at Thomas. "He's just getting settled upstairs."

Thomas nodded as the women left the room.

In the privacy of the kitchen, Mariah got straight to the point. "I can see why you're so torn."

Evelyn fixed her gaze on the tea tray as she arranged the cups and saucers. "I wish there was a way out of this that didn't hurt anyone."

"Of course you do. But I think it's foolish to assume they don't both already know how you truly feel."

Evelyn's head snapped up, her eyes wide.

Mariah smiled. "It's obvious."

"What is?"

"It's Will. It's always been him, hasn't it?"

Evelyn didn't want to answer. The truth was safer inside her. But Mariah was right, and Evelyn obviously hadn't hidden it as well as she'd thought. "Yes."

"It's nothing to be embarrassed about. We don't choose our soulmates."

Mariah was so matter-of-fact when she said it that Evelyn couldn't believe she'd never simplified the situation in such a way herself. She wasn't responsible for the chemistry she had with Will or for the fact that it surpassed the chemistry she and Thomas shared. If only that were a sufficient explanation for shattering someone's entire world.

As though reading Evelyn's mind, Mariah added, "If I may impart a piece of advice; you've been granted a second chance at being with the person you *know* is meant for you. You can search the rest of your life for that kind of connection and you won't find it again. It's worth sacrificing for."

"What if Will can't stay here?"

"Would you suddenly love Thomas more if Will left?"

Evelyn was stunned. It was such an uncomplicated question, but the truthful answer had soul-crushing ramifications.

Evelyn remembered the urn. "Wait! I need you to give Will something for me. Please." She reached into her bag and pulled out the remains of Will's mother. "I don't want to give it to him in front of Thomas."

Mariah put the tray down on the counter and took the urn, her forehead wrinkled in confusion. "Is this . . .?"

"His mother. I went to 2006 and retrieved it for him while he was asleep."

Mariah nodded and quietly put the urn on the counter. She picked up the tea tray and started for the door. "I think we've kept them waiting long enough, don't you?"

Chapter 42
1922

Evelyn had left Will in Mariah's care and Thomas had gone back to his own house for the night. She'd tried to talk him into dinner so she could break things off, but to her dismay, he'd declined. She was by herself for the first time in days, and the silence was somewhat eerie. She'd preferred Will to keep her company. The fact that he was a few blocks away and she still couldn't be with him or talk to him made her heart ache more than when he'd been eighty-four years away.

Evelyn was taken out of her thoughts by a knock at the door. Edward was standing outside with Holstead. "Good day. The doctor is here to see you."

"What a surprise! Thank you, Edward." She moved aside to let Holstead in. Edward tipped his hat and made his way back down the hall.

"I was actually planning on coming to see you today." Evelyn took Holstead's coat, forcing a smile. She was well aware that if Holstead was paying her an unscheduled visit, he was probably bearing bad news.

"Yes, I hope you don't mind the intrusion. I thought you might want to hear what I've discovered in the research files."

Her stomach dropped. Her mind instantly jumped to Will having to leave her and go back to 2006 forever. Or being in harm's way if he stayed here. She wanted the news to be anything but that. "Yes, I've been meaning to drop by and ask you if you'd found anything. I've been . . . busy."

"It can't be easy, having both Thomas and Will here."

"No."

"I'm afraid what I have to tell you won't make that conundrum any easier."

Evelyn froze. "How so?"

"Let's sit."

They took a seat in her living room. Evelyn smoothed her skirt, attempting to appear patient, but inside she was longing for Holstead to come out with it already.

He took his time sitting down before he finally spoke.

"When we first met, you came to me for answers about your abilities. Even then, it seemed you were more in tune with the dreams than any of the dreamers I'd encountered. So now, tasked with unraveling the mystery of transporting another human being from an alternate timeline, I find myself stuck, because what applied to the other dreamers may not be true for you."

Evelyn perked up. Holstead held up a finger to stop her from interrupting. "That said, there is no way to know for sure what you can withstand. And since no one, to my knowledge, has ever transported a non-dreamer before, I think it's relatively safe to say Will's wellbeing can't be promised in any of the possible scenarios in which this could all play out."

She shook her head. "What are you saying?"

"I had some trouble coming to any conclusions about Will's future here. It's unprecedented. At least in my experience. Finally, I started studying each dreamer individually, and it dawned on me that the dreamer who originally alerted Fletch to the flashes, the one with the pocket watch, might be the key to figuring this all out." Evelyn nodded, wishing he would get to the point already. "When I read through his file, I found out that the dreamer, Louis, eventually used the pocket watch to transport his pet dog to this timeline. It was the one thing he missed more than anything and he was desperate to get it back. He was successful, but once the animal was here, Louis found he couldn't travel back to his other timeline anymore. He made it there and back once or twice, but one day he simply couldn't do it. Fletch hypothesized that Louis keeping the dog here was draining all the power he previously used to travel between lives."

Evelyn furrowed her brow, the wheels in her head turning as she figured out what it all meant for her. "So, you're saying the thing keeping Will here safely . . . is me?"

"Yes."

"And the longer he's here, the less I'll be able to travel back to 2006?"

"Correct."

"And . . . there's no way to safely get him back to his own timeline?"

"Not that we know of."

A cascade of feelings hit Evelyn when she heard Will would be staying, and though she hesitated to admit it, the most overwhelming one was elation. She didn't want to seem insensitive to Thomas's position in all this, and she also felt for Will, who was about to find out he was never going back home. It was a complex set of circumstances, and she was certain it was going to get even worse before it got better.

Holstead must have read the throng of emotions on her face. "I understand you're in a difficult position. I wouldn't wish it on anyone."

Evelyn clasped her hands in her lap. "One thing still hasn't changed in spite of this information. The only way to follow my heart is to break someone else's."

Holstead shrugged. "As much as I love you and Thomas together, and you know I do, I think it would be a tragedy if you chose to spend your life with him and the entire time your heart and soul were elsewhere." He paused. "Thomas is strong. He'll recover."

Evelyn was surprised that even Holstead had caught on to her affection for Will. "I love Thomas. I really do."

"No one doubts that. We can all see how much you adore Thomas. However, I think you might find this is one of those times in life where loving someone means letting them go. In the end it will hurt him less than spending his life knowing he was your second choice."

That stung. Evelyn had never thought of Thomas as her second choice. She didn't want him to think of himself that way, either. "If I'd known there was a chance Will would come back into my life, I never would have let things get so far with Thomas. I never would have agreed to marry him! I must be the worst person in the world."

"Evelyn, you've done nothing wrong. You couldn't have predicted any of this."

"Trust me, I could have handled the entire thing better. He deserves more."

"Well, far be it from me to tell you what to do with your love life, but now that you have the answers, it's up to you to decide how to proceed."

"Thank you."

"It's my pleasure." Holstead stood up to leave. "I do hope I haven't made things more difficult on you."

Evelyn threw her hands up. "Everything about this situation is difficult! I'll manage it."

Holstead nodded. "I must be going. I'll see you soon, I'm sure."

"I'm sure." Evelyn stood and walked him to the door. Once he'd left, she was uneasy and uncertain what to do in the moment. The information was too much to process. There was only one thing she could think to do to release all her nervous energy. She hurried into her bedroom and retrieved her journal.

What do you do when your dreams come true, but your reality makes it so bittersweet you're not sure you can let yourself lean into them? It turns out Will is going to be here, in this life, for good. It's everything I've wanted deep down since I left him back in 2003, and now that I have it, I'm absolutely terrified to embrace it because to grab onto my own happiness, I have to destroy someone else's life.

Am I a good person? If I choose Will and break Thomas in two, does that make me selfish? Or does it simply make me human? It seems so easy in theory: go after the love of your life. Chase your happily ever after. But at what cost?

The truth of the matter is that Will would be stuck here even if I did choose Thomas, and as long as I know he's accessible to me, I'll never be able to give myself fully to my marriage with Thomas the way he deserves. It will ultimately come down to which one is the better match for me and which one my heart desires more. Thomas loves me and means well, but he is always practical and sensible first. Will knows how to fix my heart.

I know what I need to do. And the time has come.

Chapter 43

1922

Will was far more comfortable at Mariah's house than he had been at Thomas's place, but the hours passed slowly when he wasn't with Evelyn, no matter where he was. They'd dragged on relentlessly in his own timeline ever since she died. Every day without her had been an endless exercise in grief management.

In his room on the second floor of the Fletchers' home, Will leaned against the dresser and stared at his mother's urn, which he'd placed in the middle of the table in the sitting area. He couldn't believe Evelyn had risked everything to get it for him. They hadn't had a chance to talk about it, but more importantly, he still hadn't had a chance to thank her. He could have left every worldly possession in 2006 and never thought about it again, but his mother's remains weren't like everything else. His chest tightened as he remembered Lynn's last wishes. She wanted her ashes to be placed in the columbarium back in Ohio, next to his father's. Since she'd passed away, Will hadn't been able to bring himself to take the urn to Ohio. He'd wanted her with him. He swallowed and fought back tears over his own weakness. Evelyn had made a huge sacrifice to bring the urn to him here in 1922, but his father's ashes were sitting alone, waiting for Lynn to be with him, in 2006. He wished he'd carried out her wishes before any of this had happened, but it was too late now. The urns would never be together. He promised himself he wouldn't tell Evelyn. She'd been so selfless in going to retrieve it, and he didn't want her to feel guilty or risk going back to the other timeline to take the urn to Ohio.

A light tap on the door surprised him. It cracked open and Mariah's face poked through. "I just wanted to check and see if you needed anything."

"Nothing I can think of, thank you."

Mariah was too astute to miss his clenched jaw and tight shoulders. She stepped into the room. "I don't mean to pry, but are you all right?"

Will rubbed his hands over his face, embarrassed. "This is all just . . . a little overwhelming."

Mariah glanced at the urn on the table. "How did she pass?"

"Pneumonia. It was very unexpected."

"I'm sorry to hear that." She sat down in one of the armchairs. "You must miss her very much."

Will bit his lip and nodded.

"Evelyn took a great risk going back to get that for you."

Will was quiet as he considered how dangerous a trip Evelyn had taken and how lucky they all were that she'd made it back unscathed. "She shouldn't have gone. I feel responsible."

"Evelyn is a headstrong woman. She makes her own decisions."

"She could have been hurt. There's a madwoman on the other side who is literally trying to hunt me down. Evelyn shouldn't have gone there without me."

"She can't take you there. You're here now. She wanted to prove her love to you by going to fetch the urn. Accept the gesture and move forward."

"What if she tries to travel again?"

"We'll talk to her and make her agree not to."

Will laughed. "You said it yourself. Evelyn is headstrong. If she wants to do something, she's gonna do it."

Mariah shook her head slowly. "No. She won't. And do you know why?"

"Why?"

"Because she won't risk losing you again."

He pondered that for a moment. "And what about Thomas?"

Mariah stood and came over to Will, putting her hand on his shoulder. "I may have missed much of her life, but I know one thing about my daughter: she knows what she wants, and she goes after it. She's been that way since she was tiny."

"And you think she wants me?"

"I don't know many people who would go to the lengths she has just to catch a fleeting glimpse of someone. Surely that must tell you something." Will swallowed as Mariah turned and left the room. She stopped and turned back before she closed the door. "If you think of anything you need, I'm just down the hall." The door closed.

Alone again, Will picked up the urn and ran his fingers gently over his mother's engraved name. "That's the exact advice you would have given me, isn't it?"

A few blocks away, Evelyn had been dying to see Will all day. After Holstead left her apartment and she'd finished writing in her journal, she got ready and headed for Mariah's house where she was to spend the afternoon. She was due to meet Thomas for dinner that evening and planned to tell him she'd confirmed once and for all that Will wouldn't be going back to the other timeline, and she wasn't looking forward to his reaction. Even if he handled it calmly, inside he'd be raging, and it tore her apart to know she would be the reason for his torment. She also still had some other things to tell him that she had an inkling *would* elicit a strong outward reaction, and she was deeply apprehensive about all of it. She wanted a nice, calming few hours before she had to see him.

When Evelyn arrived, Mariah took a moment to check in on her as she took her coat and showed her inside. "How are you feeling about everything today? Any clearer?"

"Among other things, I still feel awful for accidentally bringing Will to this timeline and ripping away everything he knew, only to get here and be moved from house to house while we figure out what to do with him."

Will's voice interrupted their conversation. "I forgive you."

Evelyn clamped her hand over her mouth. Will finished coming down the stairs to join them.

He tenderly removed Evelyn's hand from her face and lowered it. "Obviously I would prefer if we could be together in the other timeline. Ideally, you never would have left. But I would move my life to *any* place, any time, for you. You know that, don't you?"

Evelyn's face turned red. She glanced at Mariah, who was staring at Will, impressed by his bold proclamation in front of her. She raised her eyebrows at Evelyn, prompting her to respond to Will, before she turned and went to the kitchen, leaving the two alone.

Evelyn turned to face him. "Will, I—"

"Wait. I have to say something to you first."

"What is it?"

"Thank you."

"For what?"

"The urn."

"You're welcome. I'm sorry I went behind your back to get it."

"I wouldn't expect anything less from you. But please don't do it again." He kissed her forehead softly.

The gentle touch of his lips made her whole body tingle. His presence was like a warm blanket. Wrapped in it, she felt secure and safe, like nothing could hurt her. His love made her invincible.

She pulled back to tell him the rest. "I saw Cammie while I was there."

His eyes widened. "You did?"

"Yes." She smiled at the memory of spending some time with her best friend. "I told her where you are and what happened. That you're okay."

"So she knows about the dreams?"

"I told her. And she was surprisingly receptive."

Will nodded. "Did you talk to her about . . . ?"

"About you and her? Yes. It's fine, don't worry."

"Oh. Are you sure?"

"I'm sure. I promise."

"Okay."

Evelyn changed the subject. "I also talked to Holstead today."

"Come on, let's go in here." He led her into the sitting room, and they sat beside each other on the sofa. "What did Holstead say?"

She stared directly into his eyes, afraid to tell him. "He said there's no way to get you back home. At least not that we know of. Holstead says my dreamer abilities are the thing keeping you here safely, but there's no way for us to go back without a huge risk to us both. I'm so sorry, Will."

His eyes were trained on the floor for a long while before he said anything. Evelyn's heart pounded as she waited for him to give her any hint of how he felt about being trapped in the 1920s for good. Finally, he met her gaze. "I'm going to need help. Setting up a life here from scratch won't be easy."

"I'll help you! Every step of the way! We all will."

"Evelyn—"

"We'll get you clothes and a job, and then we can figure out everything else. Maybe—"

"Evelyn!"

She inhaled sharply.

He continued. "I'm going to be okay." He was reaching across, holding her hand. "We'll figure it all out. First, let's talk about you."

"Me?"

"I can't imagine Thomas is going to be over the moon about the news that I can't go back," Will said. "How are we going to reassure him that I won't become a problem in your relationship with him? I don't get the sense he trusts me very much when it comes to you."

"It's me he doesn't trust. And who can blame him?"

"You haven't told him about us kissing, have you?"

"Not yet. But I'm going to. Tonight." She licked her lips before she added, "I'm going to tell him I want to break things off for good."

He sighed. "I never meant to interfere with your happiness here."

Evelyn shook her head fervently. "Will, not for a second have I ever blamed you for any of this! I'm the one who started the whole thing by flashing forward when I shouldn't have. For chasing after Cecil. Thomas is right not to trust me."

"He cares about you. A lot."

"I know."

"And I know you care about him, too. Don't do anything you'll regret."

"It's not the same!" Evelyn was surprised at her own volume. More quietly, she added, "I do love him. It's just . . . so different with you."

Just then, Mariah entered the room. "I've made some sandwiches, if you're hungry?"

Secretly frustrated at being interrupted, Evelyn and Will graciously stood and followed her to the dining room for a light lunch. Evelyn had a few hours before she had to head out to meet Thomas.

After lunch, Mariah suggested a game of cards. "I haven't played with anyone in ages! I've been dying to awe someone with my unexpected talent for bridge!"

The three sat at the table for the afternoon playing cards, laughing and forgetting everything else for a little while. Evelyn found herself completely at ease as the woman she now knew as her mother and the man she loved more than anything surrounded her in peace. It was something Evelyn hadn't experienced before. A total sense of family. No secrets, no strange disconnects. She didn't want it to end.

When it was time for her to leave, Evelyn found it difficult to part with Will. Mariah left them alone at the front door to say their goodbyes.

They faced each other, her hand on the door handle but not engaging it. "I'll come back tomorrow." It was almost a question.

"I can't wait." He didn't want her to leave anymore than she did. She missed the time when they were together in 2003, and they could spend nights together freely. When she was only his. Her body was aching to stay.

She raised herself up on her toes and gave him a light peck on the cheek before she hurried out into the city, leaving him longing for her once more.

Chapter 44
1922

Thomas was waiting for Evelyn at his office. She'd asked him to have dinner with her since they'd had little time alone lately and had so much to discuss. She planned to tell Thomas the truth that night about kissing Will and about her final decision to be with him. It was only fair to let Thomas go before she caused him anymore pain.

He greeted her with a light hug and a kiss on the cheek. As they walked down the block toward the restaurant, Evelyn noted he didn't reach for her hand. He always held her hand when they walked. It made her uneasy, like he already somehow knew she was going to let him down. She didn't reach for his hand, either.

"How was your day?" she asked. Small talk had never been her specialty.

"Not bad. Karl found a great price on some electric lighting. I was worried it would cost too much, but it looks like we'll be fully modern." He didn't sound very excited.

"That's wonderful news."

"Yes."

They walked the rest of the way in silence. By the time they were seated at dinner, Evelyn's palms were clammy. There was so much at stake on this date, and she wasn't sure she could make it through a three-course dinner without getting to the point. She would make an effort, for his sake. "I'm proud of you."

He wrinkled his forehead. "For what?"

"The office is coming along so well. You're making your dreams come true. That's something to be proud of."

He chuckled nervously and shifted in his seat. "Thank you. It certainly hasn't been easy."

"No."

"Thank you for being so patient with me while I've been working so much."

"I'm not sure how patient I've actually been."

He took a sip of water. "Of course it hasn't been all smooth sailing, but you know I'm doing this for us."

She paused, contemplating how to word her response, then cleared her throat so her voice didn't shake when she finally spoke. "There hasn't been much of an 'us' for a while."

He stiffened. Her response had activated his defenses. It was a few long seconds before he said anything. "Okay, look, I understand it's been difficult. I've been gone a lot. You've been handling things on the home front. I haven't been perfect, and I admit that. I'm sorry." He sat back in his chair and put his hands up in mock defeat.

She took a deep breath and closed her eyes. When she opened them, she still wasn't sure she'd formulated a good enough reply. "It's not just you who hasn't been perfect."

He cocked his head, interested to hear the rest.

"I have to tell you something."

"I knew it."

"Knew what? I haven't even said what it is yet!"

"It's got something to do with Will. I'd bet on it."

She clenched her jaw. She was ready to deliver what she was sure would be the fatal blow to their relationship. "Fine, it has something to do with Will."

He stared at her, his face blank.

"Since this whole thing began, with the flashes . . . I—"

"Just say it, Evelyn."

She bit her lower lip. "I kissed Will." As soon as the words were off her tongue she was filled with contrition and remorse. But notably, not with regret.

The corners of Thomas's mouth twitched as he searched for words. His hand, resting on the table, balled up into a fist. He was holding back. She was grateful but also wished he'd just lash out for once and tell her how he really felt. She was exhausted from years of having to be proper and reserved, even in their most heated moments, and she sometimes yearned to unleash the 2003 version of herself on him. She wanted to see him raw and untamed. Real.

He finally spoke. "What else?"

"What?"

"What else do you have to tell me? I'm sure there's more." The calmness in his voice was unsettling.

She squared her shoulders. "Well, you already know I went to 2006 again. Without telling anyone."

"Yes. Why would you do something so foolish?"

"I had my reasons, Thomas. And don't call me foolish."

"I'm not. What you *did* was foolish. And you know it."

"I got back here fine. There was no harm done."

"You're lucky there was no harm done! You could have been stuck there, or worse!"

"I know. I'm sorry."

He leaned back and stared at the ceiling. A few seconds passed before he looked at her again. "Is there more?"

"Holstead came by today. He told me Will can't go back to 2006. I probably can't, either."

"I see."

"You see?"

"So there are no more surprises awaiting us, then. The dreams are over now, aren't they? You can't travel anymore."

"As far as I know."

"Hmm." He fidgeted with his napkin, deep in thought.

"I never meant to hurt you," she said quietly.

"It seems if I'm going to be with you, I'll have to get used to hurting."

She snapped her head up, shocked at the idea that he still wanted to be with her at all after her string of confessions. She'd assumed they'd be the tipping point for Thomas. "I don't want that for you. I—"

"Let me decide what I can handle." He didn't sound angry.

She didn't try to finish her sentence. She was confused and exhausted. He obviously didn't want to hash everything out in the middle of a restaurant, so she followed his lead and simply nodded. She sighed and sat back in her chair. She would have to wait until later to break up with him.

He picked up his menu and forced a smile. "So, what looks good tonight?"

Chapter 45

1922

After dinner, Thomas walked Evelyn to her building as he always did. They'd had a tense meal and managed to avoid any public blowups, but Evelyn still wasn't sure how he felt about her confessions. She assumed he was upset but that he'd chosen to hide his reaction and instead only berate her about traveling to 2006. If he was quelling his emotions, she foresaw an eruption coming. She wished she'd broken things off sooner. Now she wasn't sure exactly how to bring up the conversation again, but her skin was crawling with her desperation to get out of the situation once and for all.

He took her hand as they walked. He held on limply, not fully committing, and it broke her heart a little. Even though she was planning on letting him go, the end was still painful. "Is there anything else you want to talk about?" she asked, eager to restart the discussion he'd ended so abruptly at the restaurant.

It was a few moments before he answered. "Actually, since you made your confessions, I admit I have some things I have been sitting on, myself."

Evelyn's heart skipped a beat. He had been acting strangely of late, but she'd always assumed it had to do with the stress of opening the office. She'd never even considered that Thomas would have his own secrets. "You can tell me."

He drew a sharp breath and exhaled before he began. "I am having some . . . trouble. At work. I was hoping not to worry you about it, but it turns out it might affect both of us after all, so I suppose I should finally come clean."

Evelyn was flabbergasted. After all the flak he'd given her all night about not sharing information, this sounded like something he probably should have mentioned. "What is it?"

"When I first got the office space, everything looked great. We hired the construction company, and in the beginning, the renovations were going well. Then they started doing demolition on the back part of the office and found a ton of issues. The cost of the renovation went up, and then up again."

Evelyn listened, silent, as they walked. He seemed to be waiting for her to say something, but she simply waited for him to carry on.

"Anyway, the reno bills kept piling up, and I had to find more money. After all, I couldn't just stop the project halfway through. And, well—"

She let go of his hand and stopped walking. She turned to face him, exasperated. "What is it?"

He stood in front of her, unable to look her in the eye. "I had to take out a second mortgage on my family's house, and now I might lose it."

Evelyn's jaw dropped and her eyebrows raised as far up as they could go. "You might lose your *house*?"

Thomas shushed her, looking around to make sure no one had heard. "Please, not so loud!"

She folded her arms and faced away from him for a moment to collect her thoughts. She turned to him again. "How much debt are you in?"

"It's hard to put a number on it right now. More things keep popping up every day the builders are on site."

She closed her eyes. "Please, Thomas, just get to the point."

"If I can't pay the bank back in a few weeks, they'll foreclose on the house."

She was speechless for several seconds, staring at the sidewalk as she contemplated what to say. "Does your mother know?"

"No. But the absolute worst thing that could happen is that I have to give up the house. I would still open the business as planned and start making a profit. Then I could buy us a new house, eventually."

"Thomas, this sounds risky. You and your mother could end up homeless!"

"Not homeless, just in a different, smaller home."

Evelyn exhaled hard through her nose. She was beginning to understand why he'd wanted to tell her so badly. She was also quickly putting together the plethora of financial issues that would plague them when it came to finding a new home if Thomas's house was foreclosed on. He wouldn't be able to secure a new apartment, and being a woman, neither would she. Her blood began to boil as she realized why Thomas had been trying to get her to sublet her apartment. She wondered if he would admit it out loud. "So if this all happened, you would have to find another place for your mother. Which means . . ."

"She'd probably have to come and live with us for a while, yes."

"I see." Evelyn loved Nancy Allen and cherished her time with her future mother-in-law, but she'd never envisioned them all living together. At least not until Mrs. Allen was much older. Knowing Nancy the way she did, Evelyn doubted she would want that, either. "So this is why you wanted a place with a second bedroom. Not for a baby. For your mother."

Thomas's face fell. "Yes." His voice was barely audible. "I'm sorry I didn't tell you the truth."

"I've been running around the city looking for a home for us thinking it was because you wanted a family with me, meanwhile it was all because you had a life-changing secret?"

"I suppose we've all been keeping secrets lately," he snapped back.

That stung a bit, but he wasn't wrong. Evelyn began walking again, and he followed. She didn't want to belittle him about his business dealings, but she was concerned about the long-term implications for all of them if this situation went south and furious with him for keeping it from her. They walked without talking, Thomas's shoulders slumped in shame. This had suddenly become the very worst moment to break his heart, and in spite of her earlier resolve, she simply couldn't bring herself to do it.

When he dropped her off, their goodbye wasn't as warm and loving as they had been in the past, but neither of them was surprised, given the slew of ugly truths they'd revealed during their date. As she made her way up to her apartment, Evelyn's sadness grew. As much as she wanted Will, the idea of a life without Thomas in it was scary and upsetting. He had been her rock for over three years and held her up in her most trying times. They'd built something unique and special together, and she'd never meant to cause any damage to their foundation. She'd also never expected the earthquake that was Will to come through, rocking their world to its core, and she, powerless to fight it.

Inside her apartment, she couldn't slow down the rush of thoughts in her head. She picked up her journal and sat on her bed to write.

Everything is about to come crashing down. I was going to break up with Thomas tonight, but he shocked me with some confessions of his own. It shouldn't comfort me that Thomas has also kept big secrets from me all along, but it is a relief that I'm not the only one who isn't perfect. It doesn't excuse anything I've done, or any of the things I hid from him. I still owed him more than kissing Will or chasing after Cecil behind his back. Thomas's infidelities were of the financial type. Mine were of the heart and so much worse. Admittedly, this development does make it much easier for me to walk away.

My intuition is telling me Thomas would be pulling away right now even if it weren't for the money problems he's having. If I were him, I can't say I'd have stuck around even this long.

As devastating as the idea of leaving Thomas behind is, once I do it, I have nothing stopping me from pursuing the happily ever after I always dreamed about with Will. The ending I never thought possible is right in front of me.

It's incredibly frustrating that the right moment hasn't presented itself yet, and I know when it does, it will burn down what little is left of Thomas's world.

But I'm going to do it anyway.

Chapter 46

1922

After a fitful night's sleep, Evelyn spent the next morning in menswear stores shopping for clothing to bring to Will. She desperately wanted him to be able to leave the confines of Mariah's house and explore the city—preferably with her—but he needed to blend in, and not wearing Thomas's clothes. She selected a few items that would pair together in a multitude of ways, as well as some undergarments, socks, and a hat. The store clerks repeatedly assumed the items were for Evelyn's husband, and she blushed every time she played along. They couldn't possibly know that Evelyn's shaky engagement was rapidly stumbling toward its grave. She didn't correct them and continued shopping for clothes she thought would look handsome on Will.

When she arrived at Mariah's house, Evelyn couldn't get through the front door fast enough. The sight of Will's face instantly lifted her spirits when he came down the stairs to greet her. Mariah made a show of having something to do in another part of the house and left them alone. They moved to the sitting room, where Evelyn laid out the clothing she'd bought on the chairs for him to look at.

She draped a pair of pants carefully over the back of an armchair. "These should be fine for every day. You can wear them anywhere, really. They're made with a thick wool, so they'll keep you warm—" She stopped talking when he walked over to the door and swung it closed.

"What are you doing?"

"How did it go with Thomas last night? Are you still together?"

"Well, technically, yes. He . . . admitted some things to me that derailed my plans."

He turned to face her. "I have to be honest with you because I'm going crazy." He crossed the room and stood within arm's reach of her. "Since you left yesterday, I haven't been able to stop thinking about you."

Her breath immediately became unsteady. "I've been thinking about you, too."

"I don't know how much longer I can resist kissing you again. I know it's not right, but it's the truth. This is torture."

"I know." She was frozen to the spot. Her body was urging her to go to him and give in to the love burning between them, but her mind told her she had to end things with Thomas before she could allow herself to surrender to Will again.

"I don't want you to feel obligated to be with me," he said, his eyes trained on hers. "I can go my own way somewhere else and let you and Thomas live the life you were meant to live here in the city."

"What? Will, no! I brought you here. I'm not going to leave you alone!"

"But I would! All I want is for you to be happy. I'm just afraid I'm not a good enough or strong enough person to stand here and see it with my own eyes if it's not with me."

Evelyn felt like the wind had been knocked out of her. The idea of Will simply leaving the city and starting a life without her, here in the same timeline where they'd always know the other was just within reach, was her idea of hell on earth. She recalled Thomas's bombshell confession the night before. "Things between Thomas and me are . . . fragile . . . at the moment."

"I can imagine."

"No, there's more than you even know. Obviously things with you and me are causing tension, but there are some things Thomas has done that have also contributed to where we are now." She fidgeted with the pants hanging on the chair. "I really did mean to end things last night, but I couldn't do it."

"I'm really sorry. I mean it. I hate to see you hurting. And Thomas is a good guy. He should be happy, too."

Her eyes caught his, and she stared at him, the wheels in her head turning. "What would we do?"

"What do you mean?"

"You and me. If we were together. *Really* together. Here, in this timeline. What would we do? Tell me how you envision our life together."

The question caught him off guard. He considered his answer for a few seconds, not taking his eyes off her. "We'll start over. Anywhere. We'll get married as soon as we can, and we'll find a place to live. I'll get a job, and you can work as much or as little as you want to. We'll go on dates, and we'll walk along our street holding hands every evening while you make me laugh and it lights up every part of my soul. The way you always do. The way you always have." He gently tipped her chin up toward him with his fingertips. "I'll make dinner for you because you're a terrible cook, and I love that about you. We'll go on trips. Walk along beaches. We'll watch sunsets, and on mornings when we're not still fast asleep wrapped in each other's arms, we'll watch the sunrise, too. We'll visit boring museums and be the only ones who enjoy them. Explore new cities together. We'll come home and wish we were still traveling the world, but we'll be just as happy in our little house together, because being with you is like taking a trip every day through the bravest, most impressive, and most brilliant mind I've ever known." He lovingly held her shoulders in his hands, his fingers warm on her skin. "You'll never have to hide anything from me. Not your dreams, not anything. I'll be your partner. There won't be anything we can't fight our way through. We'll have a family, or maybe we won't, but either way, it'll be the most amazing, beautiful adventure I've ever been on, and I will never, ever want to be anywhere else but by your side." Will lowered his hands and took hers. "We'll grow old together, and when we do, you will still be the reason I wake up every morning until the day I don't wake up at all. Then I'll wait for you on the other side. As long as it takes. And when we're finally together again, we'll make another love story, in another world, where nothing can ever tear us apart again. *That's* the happy ending I want."

She grabbed his face and pulled his mouth to hers, releasing all the pent-up passion from within. His answer had awoken something fervent inside her, and everything was telling her it wasn't going to go back to sleep. When they pulled back, he swallowed hard and they stared at each other, breathless. Evelyn broke the silence. "I have to end things with Thomas. Today."

Chapter 47

1922

Inside Evelyn's apartment that evening, Thomas hung up his hat and coat and sat down on the sofa. Evelyn sat next to him. After an uncomfortably long pause, she started the conversation they'd both been dreading for weeks. "What are we doing, Thomas?"

He didn't answer. His eyes were plastered on the floor in front of him.

She continued. "We can't go on this way. Things between us have been uncertain for a long time, and with everything that's happened in the last couple of weeks, it's just . . ." She threw her hands up, unable to complete her sentence.

"I know." He didn't look up.

"I love you. I do. But I don't think love is enough for us." She couldn't help the tears that were forming in her eyes.

He swallowed the painful lump in his throat. "I love you, too," he whispered.

She took his hand. "I'm sorry." She paused to fight the tears. In spite of her efforts, they were now rolling down her cheeks. "You and I started off so well. I don't know where we got lost. I'm so sorry I didn't find my way back."

He shook his head, squeezing his eyes shut to keep from crying. "I should have given you more of my time. My attention. I let the business come between us. I never wanted you to feel like I wasn't there or like I didn't want to be. I was doing it for us, but I got too invested. I lost sight of you."

"It's my fault, too. I shouldn't have chased down Cecil or flashed forward. I should have focused on you, too."

Thomas finally looked up. It was a few seconds before he spoke. "You and I met exactly when we were supposed to. You brought me out of my shell. Out of my library. You opened my eyes to love, Evelyn. You were the reason I was so driven to become a doctor, to start my own practice, to succeed! I would never have the fire in me that I do now if it hadn't been for you. I'll never be able to thank you for that. You changed me." He took a breath before he continued. "But . . . you and Will have crossed *worlds* to be together. You've found each other no matter where you've been, or when. It is physically painful for me to say this out loud, but it's *so* clear that he's the one you're meant to be with. I can't stand in the way of that. I never would."

"Thomas, I—"

"No! Evelyn, don't. I've seen the way you light up when he's around. You couldn't hide your joy when you found out he might not be able to return to his own life. I've noticed how you look at him when he comes into the room. Your eyes . . . they don't sparkle like that for me. They never have."

She doubled over, crying, still holding his hand. He tenderly rubbed her upper arm. "Please don't feel guilty. I'm not angry with you. I'll be fine." Tears were now falling from his own eyes.

She sat up and used her handkerchief to dry her face, sniffling. "I never wanted it to end like this."

"I never wanted it to end."

"I'll always love you. You've been my best friend for a long time."

"I'll love you until the day I die, Evelyn Moore."

"What will you do now?"

"Whatever it takes to fix my mess."

She looked down at her hands. "Oh! The ring . . ." She pulled it off her finger and stared at it between her fingertips, still glittering, ignorant that the love it represented was dying an agonizing death. She held it out to him.

He let out a sniffle as he took it from her hand, closing his fist around it. He looked at her and clenched his jaw. "No." He opened his palm and held the ring back out to her. "You keep it."

"What? No, I can't."

"It's worth a little bit of money. Use it to start your life with Will. Please. I can't take the ring back, Evelyn. It's too painful." Evelyn could see how hard he was holding back from expressing all his emotions in front of her.

"Won't you need it someday? You know, if you find someone else to—"

"Please. Don't finish that sentence. Not now. You have to take the ring."

She slowly reached out and picked it up out of his hand. He let out a shaky gasp as she did.

She ran her fingertips over the metal of the ring, still warm from being on her finger, now an unlikely symbol of both her past and her future. "I don't know what to say."

"Don't say anything." He gently pushed her fingers closed around the ring and held her fist in his hands. He raised it up to his lips and kissed her hand softly. "I have to go." He let go of her and stood up.

"Will I see you again?"

He wiped his face dry and gazed down at her, a small smile forming on the edges of his mouth. "I hope someday I'm strong enough for that."

He turned and headed for the door. Giving her one final glance, he closed it behind him, leaving a heartbroken Evelyn on her sofa, clutching the ring and crying so hard it hurt.

A while later, she sat up and dried her eyes. She gathered herself and splashed her face with cold water in the kitchen before she went into her bedroom and retrieved her journal. On her bed, she flipped the book open to the first blank page. She began writing in the very center.

Part II: My Happily Ever After

Epilogue

1923, Great Neck, Long Island, New York

The beach was quiet at sunset, which was just the way Evelyn liked it. As the sky morphed from its end-of-summer blue to a colorful swirl, she breathed in the salty air and watched a seagull soaring overhead. This had quickly and easily become her favorite time of day.

She walked slowly along the edge of the water, letting the waves trickle over her feet when they made it that far, and wondered how everyone in the city was doing. She'd had a letter recently from Ada, who said she was coming out for a visit over Labor Day weekend. Evelyn couldn't wait to see her. Since she'd moved out of Manhattan, she'd seen little of Ada, Holstead, or Mariah and promised herself she'd make a trip to the city soon to catch up with them all.

She missed life in New York. Some days she still found herself craving the buzz of the Manhattan streets, but there was a peacefulness here next to the water that fed a part of her soul she'd never realized was starving. She could breathe here in a way she never could amid the hustle and bustle of the city. Still, she'd left a piece of her heart in New York and would never be able to leave the city behind completely.

She walked away from the water a little and sat down, pulling out her journal. She hadn't written in it since before she'd moved.

Life here is perfect. I've finally found a calm, normal existence without time traveling or magic dreams, and I couldn't be happier.

My parents in Virginia are due to come for a visit sometime around the holidays. I still haven't told them I know about Mariah and Doctor Fletcher, but I think it's better this way. They have always done what they thought was best for me, and now I'll do the same for them. They're happier thinking I still don't know about the adoption, and I don't want to ruin that.

I've also had another revelation about my past that explained so much about me being a dreamer and my biological father's obsession with the dreams. Mariah wrote to some of Fletcher's relatives and found out more about our family tree. She discovered that Fletcher's mother, Agatha, had spent her life fighting what was described in old letters as an unknown condition that caused her to "hallucinate visions of the future in her sleep." I didn't need anymore information to figure out that Fletcher labeled her "O.D." on the family tree because she is the Original Dreamer in his studies and began his obsession with the dreamers. It also explains why I'm a dreamer. I never thought I'd be able to trace it back to anything, and knowing the reason I've always been so different is extremely vindicating. It makes every time I was ever told the dreams were a delusion a distant memory.

When I think back to all the people I've met in the last few years who helped me get to where I am today, I'm overwhelmed. Strangers from two timelines quickly became some of the most important people in my entire life. I can never repay Doctor Holstead—or Caroline, especially. I'll always wonder what happened to poor Lydia back in the other timeline. It's hard to accept that I may never know if she found peace, but I truly hope she did.

I also had a letter from Thomas today. It's the first time he's written to me since we said goodbye. His practice is open, and he says it's doing well so far, and that if things stay this way, he'll be able to buy a nice home for himself and Nancy, who is also doing well in spite of being forced to move out of the house she loved.

I admit it was hard to see Thomas's name on the envelope when it arrived. I spend so much time thinking of how he might be doing since we parted ways and broke off our engagement. It still hurts that we had to end something that began with so much promise, and I hope his next letter is to tell me he's found someone who loves him the way I never could. Someone whose heart isn't a million miles—or eighty-four years—away. He deserves it. For all that happened between us, I know he was one of the most amazing people I will ever meet. Any woman would be lucky to have him.

For my part, I think I've grown a lot since moving out here. I'm working for a local attorney my old boss, Mr. Allen, introduced me to. It feels amazing to be back to work instead of frittering away my days running errands and touring apartments I could never afford. Looking back, I never should have agreed to stop working in the first place. There's a presidential election next year, and my boss says he might be able to get me a position on the campaign's volunteer staff. I haven't been involved in anything like this since before I left 2003, and I'm aching to get back out there. I need to be a part of something bigger. I always have.

"Room for one more?"

Evelyn turned to see Will jogging to meet up with her. The smile that spread across her face was completely involuntary. She reached out her hand, and he took it as he helped her to her feet. They walked together, her journal resting safely on their little stretch of beach behind them.

She pulled him closer and hugged his arm. "You almost missed it!"

"You know I'd never miss our sunset." They stopped walking and stood with their arms around each other as the sun dipped below the horizon, casting a pink glow over the water and highlighting Evelyn's face in the way Will looked forward to every day. "I still can't believe I'm here with you."

She wrapped her arms around his neck. "I can. You're the man of my dreams."

THE END

Acknowledgments

What a ride this has been. Becoming an author has gone better than I ever pictured. The idea that people have devoted their precious time, money, and emotions into Evelyn and her world is humbling beyond measure. I've been honored to share these characters with each and every one of you, and I hope you'll stay on this journey with me as I endeavor to write more books you'll love.

Thanks as always to my husband and children. To my incredibly supportive family and friends: how could I possibly do any of this without you? Immense gratitude to my editor, Jessica, whose expertise has been an integral part of these books and my education as a writer.

Until next time, dear readers. Keep dreaming.

About the Author

Laura Spivak is a new author out of Maryland, USA. When she's not writing, she's being mom to three amazing kids, wife to a dreamy husband, and working in the grant writing space. She has previously worked as a news writer and has had articles featured on a popular parenting platform. Laura is excited to get to work on writing your next favorite novel!